KU-229-924

# WEST
## OF THE
# RIMROCK

## Wayne D. Overholser

CENTER POINT LARGE PRINT
THORNDIKE, MAINE

This Center Point Large Print edition
is published in the year 2020 by arrangement with
Golden West Literary Agency.

Copyright © 1949 by Wayne D. Overholser.
Copyright © 1976 by Wayne D. Overholser.

All rights reserved.

Originally published in the US by Macmillan.

The text of this Large Print edition is unabridged.
In other aspects, this book may vary
from the original edition.

Set in 16-point Times New Roman type.

ISBN: 978-1-64358-748-6 (hardcover)
ISBN: 978-1-64358-752-3 (paperback)

The Library of Congress has cataloged this record under
Library of Congress Control Number: 2020943943

Libraries NI

| | | |
|---|---|---|
| C903506582 | | |
| W.F.HOWES | | 1/2/2022 |
| | | £20.50 |
| AHS | | |

MIX
Paper from
responsible sources
FSC® C013056

Printed and bound in Great Britain
by TJ Books Ltd, Padstow, Cornwall

To My Wife Evaleth

# Contents

1. Tar-Paper Shack      9
2. Clancy's Town      23
3. Clancys Are Stubborn      37
4. The Girl Peg      47
5. Born a Clancy      58
6. The Carricks      69
7. The Fight at Blazer's Place      88
8. The Schemes of Little Men      106
9. Short Man, Long Shadow      114
10. Clancy Ears Are Stone      127
11. Death at Turkey Track      138
12. Chase      150
13. Hideout      164
14. "Let the People Fight"      175
15. Clancy Beef for Nesters      187
16. Woman Against Woman      201
17. The Man Called Friend      210
18. The Wheel Is Turned      223
19. Search      235
20. The Trap      247
21. Land Sale      262
22. Stampede      273
23. Final Woman      287

# Chapter 1: Tar-Paper Shack

TRAVELING EASTWARD, MURDO MORGAN left the pines in mid-morning and came into the high Oregon Desert. He made a dry noon camp under a wind-turned juniper, drank sparingly from his canteen, and rode on. The sky was without clouds; the sun laid a hot pressure upon him. Sage grew in rounded clumps as far as he could see, the smell of it a desert incense in his nostrils.

He forked his black easily in the way of a man who rides much, the dust of uncounted miles upon him. His face was high-boned, his nose thin—features that had marked all the Morgans he had ever known. They had marked his father, who had left Paradise Valley sixteen years before, a broken and defeated man; they had marked his three brothers, who lay buried below the valley's east rim.

Today Morgan rode across country he did not remember; tomorrow he would be in Paradise Valley. He pictured it now with the nostalgic eagerness of a grown man returning to his boyhood home. He had long dreamed of this return, of how he would stomp Broad Clancy under his bootheels, of how he would smash Turkey

Track's hold on the valley. They had been childish dreams inspired by a boy's lust for revenge, a lust that had been blunted by the years. A different purpose had brought him back, although Broad Clancy would not believe it. There was another dream, a greater one than the boy dreams, that Murdo Morgan wanted to turn into reality.

The town of Irish Bend lay ahead, but Morgan could not guess the distance in miles. The country seemed entirely strange. It was late spring, and the desert, never really green, was feeling the surge of its scant life.

He remembered that it had been fall when he'd ridden out of the country with his father, but it was not the difference in seasons that made the desert seem unfamiliar. The years had dimmed his memory of these empty miles. At twenty-seven he retained few of the thoughts and images that had been bright in his eleven-year-old mind. Even the dream had changed and grown with time. Now it was a lodestar calling him back to risk both his life and his money.

Morgan followed an east-west valley, rimrock an unbroken line to his left. A jackrabbit broke into the open and kicked high into the air. A band of antelope raced away from Morgan to fade into the sage. In late afternoon he came to a herd of cattle carrying the Turkey Track brand, evidence that Broad Clancy's domain spread far beyond Paradise Valley.

Dusk caught him with Irish Bend still not in sight. He made camp beside a tar-paper shack, built a small fire and cooked supper. When he was done with it he kicked it out, for his was a dangerous business, and he had learned long ago that a man silhouetted against a night blaze made a good target.

Darkness folded about him, the last golden glow of sunset dying along the snowy crest of the Cascades. Morgan lay on his back, head on his saddle, eyes on the stars set in a tall sky. There was this moment when he could thrust worry away and let the dreams build, but another night would bring its sultry threat of violence. He wasn't fooling himself. He remembered Broad Clancy too well.

But this night was to be enjoyed: the desert smells, the desert wildness, the great emptiness of this land with its rimrock and buttes, its juniper and sage. It shouldn't be an empty land. The valley bottom could be irrigated, the lower slopes of the surrounding buttes dry farmed. Given normal luck and a boost from Providence, a thousand families could make a living on land that now supported only Broad Clancy's Turkey Track and a handful of settlers. That was Murdo Morgan's dream, to place a thousand families on land that would be theirs.

He gave himself to speculation about the tar-paper shack. Four walls with a broken window and no door, a roof partly stripped by the wind, a splintered floor. A few newspapers in the corner. *Portland Oregonians*, Morgan noted, not yet yellowed by age. And outside, almost covered by windblown sand, was a weather-grayed cradle. Homemade and crude, but hinting at a poignant story.

Knowing Broad Clancy, Morgan could guess the story. Clancy would tolerate only a limited number of nesters on his range and only at places he designated. His men had come here, probably late at night, routed the nesters from their bed, and started them on their way. And a baby had learned to sleep without its cradle.

The run of a horse brought Morgan upright. He listened a moment, placing the horse to the east and gauging its speed. It was coming directly toward him. Pulling saddle and blanket from the shack, he hunkered there to listen.

Another horse was coming from the south. Morgan waited, tense, not hearing the first horse for a time. Then they were both in front of the shack, and a man called, "Peg!"

Morgan heard the girl's laugh, gay and soft and compelling. She said, "You'd ride through the whole Clancy outfit to get here, wouldn't you, Buck?"

"It was a damn' fool risk," the man said irritably.

The girl laughed. "Afraid, Buck?"

"You know I ain't. I just ain't gonna stand for you playing around with Rip and egging me on at the same time. You're making up your mind tonight."

"What makes you think I see Rip?"

"There's talk enough. Is it me or Rip?"

"You men are all fools." There was the creak of saddle leather as she stepped down. "You're wasting time, Buck."

"I want to know."

"Of course it's you."

"Then I'm telling you, Peg. If I ever catch you—"

"Buck, are you going to kiss me?"

He swung out of the saddle then. Morgan saw them come together, the two shapes mold into one, heard whispers of talk that reached him as blurred sounds. From what he had heard about the valley, he guessed this would be Buck Carrick, a nester's son.

Buck flamed a match and held it to his cigarette, the glow of it making a brief brightness. He had a handsome square face, his eyes dark and widely spaced, his chin a fighter's chin. About twenty-five, Morgan guessed. Old enough to be in love and foolish enough to meet this girl at risk of his life.

Peg, for some reason Morgan hadn't heard, was suddenly angry.

"I won't ride off with you, Buck, and I didn't

have you come here for Rip to shoot. If that's the way you trust me, get on your horse and keep riding."

"I told you this was the night you were making up your mind," Buck said roughly. "You've kept me dangling for two years. I can't stand it no longer."

"Let me go," the girl cried.

"We'll get married in Prineville and we'll take the stage to The Dalles."

"Your dad will—"

"We'll be out of the country before he knows anything about it."

"You're crazy, Buck."

"That's right. Crazy with loving you. Crazy with wanting you. Crazy with worrying what Rip Clancy is doing to you. I love you, Peg. Isn't that enough?"

"No. Not nearly enough. I'll never marry you."

"You said I was the one. That's all I want to know."

Morgan had crawled through the sage to the shack. He came to his feet, gun fisted. "Let her go, Buck. It's too dark to see what you're up to, so don't make any fast moves."

The girl jerked out of Buck's arms and ran to her horse. Buck stood still, a square black shape in the starlight. He asked, "Who are you?"

"Makes no never mind. Mount up and git."

"I ain't leaving her with you," Buck said

doggedly. "How do I know what you're figgering on?"

"I ain't keeping the girl, but if she rides, you'll sit pat for a spell."

"Maybe I'm not in a hurry, mister," the girl said.

"Then you ain't smart."

"You're wrong on that."

"Go on."

"I hope I'll see you again."

"Don't ever see her," Buck groaned. "She'll drag you through hell. She's poison."

Peg was in the saddle now, her laugh gay and without the shadow of fear. "Why, Buck, I thought you liked my poison."

Wheeling her mount, she rode eastward. Morgan held Buck there until the sound of her horse was lost in the desert stillness. He said then: "All right, son. Remember what I said about fast moves."

"I ain't forgetting," Buck said bitterly. "Likewise I ain't forgetting what you done tonight."

"I hope you won't, because you'll thank me some day. Go on now. Vamoose."

But Buck stood motionless, as if listening. Morgan heard it then. More horses. Coming toward them.

"I didn't see anybody all day," Morgan said. "Now the desert's alive."

"It's Peg's work," Buck said with deep

sourness. "She does that to a man. She's a fever in your blood if you look at her twice. I'm warning you, mister. Stay away from her."

"Got a guess on who's coming?"

"Rip Clancy and some Turkey Track hands. Chances are Peg met 'em and headed 'em this way."

"Then you'd better make dust. I'll hold 'em off."

Buck stepped up. "You don't owe me nothing, friend. This roan I'm riding can outrun any nag they've got."

"I've got my own reason for not wanting a ruckus to bust out. Get moving. Run your horse for a few minutes. Then pull up and take it easy."

"I know a few things," Buck said resentfully. Cracking steel to his horse, he disappeared the way he had come.

Morgan remained at the shack, his back to the wall. There was no moon, and the starlight made a thin glow on the desert.

His lot had been a lonely one. No mother that he could remember. His father dead when he was twelve, nerves shattered and health broken by Broad Clancy's lead, the dream a prodding ambition until the moment of his death. That dream had been Murdo Morgan's only inheritance.

The lonely years then. A chore boy on one ranch after another. A cowhand in Montana. A lawman in tough Arizona border towns. Finally the Colorado mining camps. Then his luck had turned. He'd grubstaked a prospector and the man had struck it. That had given Morgan his stake, enough to buy the wagon-road grant that made up half of Paradise Valley.

Morgan smiled now as he thought of the Cascade & Paradise Land Company. He was that land company, but it was just as well Broad Clancy didn't know it for a time. Clancy hated the company enough. He'd hate it twice as much if he knew the company and Murdo Morgan were one and the same.

Clancy had used this range for years, government and company land alike, ignoring the fact that the odd sections of a strip six miles wide on both sides of the old wagon road belonged to the company. The company had made no effort to collect rent and Clancy had neither offered to pay nor to lease the land. With high disdain for the right of private property, he had considered all the valley land open range and had acted accordingly.

Because Morgan's life had been a lonely and womanless one, his thoughts turned to the girl Peg. He wondered what she looked like. He heard again the gay tone of her laughter. It had been a fine sound to hear. It would stay with him like a sweet haunting tune he had heard whistled.

Then his thoughts turned bitter. There had been no trouble in the valley since Morgan and his father had left. Now this Peg had Buck Carrick and Rip Clancy in love with her. It would take a woman, he thought, to stir up a feud at a moment when he was bringing trouble enough of his own.

He caught the blur of running horses. Four of them pointed directly toward the shack. Morgan wondered what kind of girl Peg was who would allow her flurry of anger to turn her from Buck to the Clancys.

They were there, then, reining up in a whirling cloud of dust that drifted toward the shack. A man in front called imperiously, "Come out of there, Carrick."

"He's gone," Morgan said. "If you boys'll keep riding, I'll go back to sleep."

"Who the hell are you?"

"Makes you no never mind, does it, friend?"

"You're on Turkey Track range. Get off."

"Reckon I'm hurting the bunchgrass? Or the sagebrush maybe?"

"Acting smart won't buy you nothing. I said to drift. This is Rip Clancy talking."

"A Clancy don't cut no bigger swath than the next man." Anger honed a fine edge to Morgan's voice. "I aim to finish my sleep."

"You'll finish it in hell if—"

"We're getting sidetracked," a gravelly-voiced rider beside Rip said. "This is just a drifter. We're after Carrick."

The man loomed a head taller than Rip and

18

wider of shoulder. Morgan could tell nothing about him beyond that, but his voice was one a man would never forget.

"Why don't you light out after Carrick?" Morgan asked. "He allowed you didn't have an animal that could run with his roan."

Rip cursed shrilly. "He's just a bragging fool. Where'd he go?"

"South."

He told them the truth and knew they wouldn't believe it. He smiled, thinking they'd look for Buck in any direction but south.

"I've got a hunch he's in the shack," Rip said uncertainly. "I'm gonna take a look."

"I wouldn't, sonny," Morgan breathed. "It's too dark to watch you real close, so I'm thinking you'd best stay where you are."

"You ain't tough enough to stop us."

"I ain't real sure about that, but I've got an iron in my hand that says I'll make a hell of a mess out of your bunch while I'm trying."

There was silence then except for the heavy breathing of the Turkey Track men. This was an old and familiar business for Murdo Morgan, but he didn't like it. Somewhere along his back trail he had lost his appetite for powder smoke. He had come here to build, not to destroy. But this was a matter of living or dying.

"What are you doing on this range?" Rip Clancy demanded.

"My business, sonny."

"It's Clancy business," Rip said arrogantly. "I'll tell you something a drifter needs to know. Around here folks do what Broad Clancy says. If they don't, they have trouble. Buck Carrick knew he was off the reservation when he came here. I think he's inside now and you're covering up for him. If we find him, we'll make wolf meat out of him."

"What's between you and Buck Carrick is nothing to me. Right now my business is to keep you on your horse."

"If Buck's inside," the big man said, "it makes two guns, and he ain't worth getting killed over. We'll wait till the sign's right, Rip."

But Rip Clancy was too young and too much in love to consider the risk. He said darkly: "There's four of us. This hairpin can't be as tough as he acts."

A smart man wouldn't have walked into it. Not with the darkness as thick as it was and with Morgan standing that way, his back to the shack wall. What light there was worked to his advantage. The gravelly-voiced man knew it. Another time Rip would have known it. But Buck Carrick had met Peg here. The bitterness rising from that thought was a potion deadening Rip's natural instinct of self-preservation.

"Too bad you're bent on committing suicide tonight," Morgan murmured. "You ought to give

20

yourself time to play your string out with Peg."

It was a long shot that might work either way. Morgan heard Rip's indrawn breath, heard him ask, "What do you know about Peg?" in a high nerve-tightened voice. Then a faint challenging cry came from the south, and a gun sounded, muffled by distance.

"That'll be Buck," the gravelly-voiced man said. "Let's get him."

Wheeling their horses, they pounded south toward the gun blast. Morgan felt his admiration for Buck Carrick. He'd waited out there in the sage to pull the Turkey Track riders off, because it was his fight and none of Murdo Morgan's. With a fast horse under him and a black night to hide in, he could play fox and hounds with a better than even chance to get clear.

Morgan built a cigarette and smoked it before he went back to his blanket. Horse sounds faded and desert emptiness was all around him again. He vaguely remembered the Clancy kids. There was Short John, older than Morgan, about fourteen when Morgan had left the valley and a runt for his age. Morgan remembered a girl named Jewell. She'd be in her early twenties now. This Rip was the youngest. He had been little more than a baby when Morgan and his father had ridden out of the country.

Then the memory of Peg's rich laugh crowded the Clancys out of Morgan's mind. He wouldn't like her. He wouldn't like any girl who played two men against each other to satisfy her own sense of feminine importance, but he'd never forget her.

# Chapter 2: Clancy's Town

IT WAS EARLY MORNING WHEN MORGAN swung to the south, put his black across the shoulder of a juniper-covered butte, and looked down into Paradise Valley, the huddle of buildings that was Irish Bend centering the flat. Beyond the town lay the dirty pool of water that was dignified by the name of Paradise Lake. South of it a patch of hay land was a bright emerald in a sage-gray setting.

Again nostalgia struck at Murdo Morgan. He and his father had paused here to blow their horses. Morgan had had his last look at the valley then. Sixteen years ago, but reality as he saw it now was a bright picture perfectly fitting the memory.

Rimrock lined the northern part of the valley. Farther east it rose into a number of jagged ridges known as the Hagerman Hills. They broke off into a series of buttes forming part of the eastern and all of the southern rim of the valley.

Clancy's Turkey Track buildings were directly below Morgan. Far across the valley was the site of the Morgan place. The sharpest picture among all the memories that had clung in his mind from that day sixteen years ago was the sight of smoke rising from the cabin. Clancy had not waited until they were out of the valley to burn it.

Morgan turned his eyes to the north. Along the edge of the lake, alkali glittered in the morning sunlight like a patch of white frost. Farther north, just under the rimrock, was another white area Broad Clancy had named Alkali Flats.

Morgan sat his saddle for a long time, bringing every detail back to his mind. Then his thoughts turned to Ed Cole. Cole was a San Francisco man Morgan had met in Colorado years before as a field representative of a land company. After he had secured his option on the wagon-road grant, he had looked Cole up and told him he was $100,000 short.

"I'm working for the Citizens' Bank now," Cole said, "and I think I can wangle a loan for you. As a matter of fact, we had been dickering for the valley ourselves, but we felt the price was a little steep."

"I'd be beholden to you," Morgan said.

"Not at all. A straight business proposition."

"Ought to be a good deal for the bank. The valley's worth five times what I'm asking to borrow."

Cole laughed. "You're an optimist, Murdo. Not many bankers would agree with you."

"Why hell, Ed, that—"

"I know." Cole held up a carefully manicured hand. "I've been there. It's good land, but it needs

24

water and lots of it. Besides, you've got Broad Clancy to buck and a shirttailful of squatters like Pete Royce at the lake and the Carricks below the east rim who won't want to move. What's more, you're a hell of a long ways from a railroad. That valley isn't worth a nickel if you don't get settlers on it. How are you going to do that?"

Morgan had an idea, but it was his notion and not Ed Cole's. Shrugging, he said, "I'll figger on it," and left Cole's office.

When the loan had been approved, Morgan had gone immediately to the office of the Gardner Land Development Company. He had never met Grant Gardner, but he had heard of him, a strange kind of capitalist who was more interested in developing farm colonies than making money.

But Grant Gardner was harder headed than Morgan had heard. "I admire your courage, Morgan," he said bluntly, "but not your business sense. You've put a fortune into that road grant and borrowed $100,000 to boot. I know the Citizens' Bank. It's run by a bunch of robbers. If you slip when the time comes to pay, you'll lose your shirt."

"I've got till October," Morgan said. "By that time I'll have the land sold."

Gardner threw up his hands. "Damn it, Morgan, you're a lamb playing with wolves. How are you going to get a thousand families into your valley by October?"

"I figgered on getting your help," Morgan admitted. "You see, I had a wild notion you were the kind of dreamer my father was. From the time I remember anything, I remember him talking about how land wears out and folks have to keep moving west. He said we had to plow up new land to support a population that keeps growing. He wanted to help the settlers when they came to Paradise Valley, but they didn't come soon enough. If I've guessed wrong, Gardner, I'll have to get a job punching cows, 'cause I sure as hell will lose my shirt."

For a long time Gardner sat in silence as he made his appraisal of Morgan, pulling steadily on his cigar, finger tips tapping his desk. He said then, "You're not wrong about me, Morgan. I'm a dreamer and a gambler to boot. I've taken some long chances on land development, and folks have called me crazy the same as I'm calling you. Maybe I am crazy, but I have a conviction that the future of the West lies in agriculture, not the cattle business. We've all got some kind of a job to do, or we wouldn't be here. Mine is to bring about the settlement of land that can be profitably farmed."

"Now you're talking my language," Morgan said.

Gardner shook his head. "Afraid not, Morgan. I said profitably farmed. I can't see that you've got a chance with your wagon-road grant. It strikes me you've been carried away by the memory of an idealist father."

"Maybe," Morgan said doggedly, "but I've seen men with guts enough to take long chances pull off some crazy-looking propositions. I'll pull this one off if I get a little help. I need a national organization to sell the land. You've got it. Would you put Paradise Valley over for 10 per cent of the sales?"

Gardner thought about it a moment before he nodded. "Yes, I'll give you that much of a boost."

"Another thing. I'll sell the bottom land in small tracts, but a farmer needs water to make a living off that kind of acreage. There are some creeks flowing into the lake that run enough water for a thousand families if we had the reservoirs to hold the runoff."

"A million dollars?"

Morgan shook his head. "I'd say half of that."

"Figure me out," Gardner said flatly. "I'm not that kind of a gambler."

"My idea is to use a lottery to sell the valley," Morgan went on.

Gardner laughed shortly. "Can't be done. The laws of the United States forbid it."

"We'll get around that by letting them bid on every piece of land after it's drawn. We'll have a government man there to see it's done the way it's supposed to be."

Gardner scratched the end of his nose. "You've

got a better head than I gave you credit for, Morgan. Tell you what I'll do. I'll sell the land for you and push the lottery idea. I'll send a crew to handle the land sale and I'll be there myself. If you've got the right kind of settlers who don't expect something for nothing, I'll put in your irrigation project."

"That's all I'm asking," Morgan said.

Morgan rose and reached the door before Gardner warned, "Don't expect any mercy from the Citizens' Bank or Ed Cole."

"I won't need it. I'll have the money."

"When do you plan the sale?"

"September 1."

Gardner nodded approval. "Good. That's time enough. Keep me informed. I'll be in Irish Bend before September 1."

So Morgan had taken his black gelding from the livery and ridden north. He thought of the warning Gardner had given him about Cole and the Citizens' Bank, but it failed to worry him. He had known Cole personally for six years, and regarded him as a friend. In any case the loan had been made, and Murdo Morgan owned the wagon-road grant. If Gardner did his selling job, the money would be on hand before October.

Now, with his eyes on the valley, a faint premonition of disaster slid along Morgan's spine like the passage of a cold snake. He would have to dispossess the nester families or talk them into buying the land they squatted on. Broad Clancy was a tougher problem. Yet Morgan held no sympathy for either the nesters or Clancy. They had stubbornly settled on land they had selected, regardless of whether it was government land open to entry or company-owned property.

A gray streak of a road cut through the sage from the north rim to Irish Bend and wound on to the south buttes, twisting a little to the west so that it ran directly toward a sharp peak rising boldly above the lesser hills. It was Clancy Mountain. Behind it, in the high country, was Clancy Marsh, Turkey Track's summer range.

It was poor graze along the north edge of the valley, with rock ridges extending like giant fingers southward from the rim. With the exception of Pete Royce at the lake and the Carricks farther east, the squatters had all located along the north edge of the valley. The bulk of the bottom land was rich with bunchgrass growing among the sage clumps, good graze, an empire worth fighting for.

Morgan put his black down the steep slope to the valley floor and, keeping north of the Turkey Track buildings, lined directly across the valley to Irish Bend. The sun climbed until it was noon high, rolling back purple shadows that clung tenaciously to the Hagerman Hills. It was a still day, utterly without wind, stiflingly hot for so early in the season.

Reaching Irish Bend shortly after noon, Morgan stabled his horse and told the hostler: "Treat him right. He's come a ways."

The hostler nodded, tight-lipped, and said nothing, but suspicion was plain to read on his long face. Morgan stepped through the archway. He stood for a moment in the sun's glare, gray eyes raking the street, a lock of black hair sweat-pasted to his forehead.

He made his appraisal of the town without hurry, taking his time building his cigarette. He had the pinched-in-the-middle look and the wide shoulders of a man who had spent most of his life in the saddle. His face and hands were tanned a dark mahogany, his clothes and holster and gun butt were black. In many ways he looked like any of the Turkey Track riders who idled along the street, yet he was a stranger and therefore set apart.

Morgan left the stable and moved toward the hotel, passing the Elite saloon and going on across the intersection made by the town's single side street. He walked with studied indifference, feeling many eyes watching from the hidden places of the town. Suspicion was here. Later, when his purpose became known, that suspicion would turn to open hostility.

A tight smile cut at the corners of his mouth. He understood this and expected it. A man who has lived with danger as a constant traveling mate develops a feeling that is close to instinct. He was like a dog setting his face toward a wolf pack, bristles up, muscles tensed. Irish Bend had been no more than a single store sixteen years ago. Now it was a cowtown supported and permitted to exist by the grace of Broad Clancy. When the time came, every hand would be against Murdo Morgan because Clancy willed it so.

That was the way it had been with Morgan. He had been looked upon with distrust before. It was never pleasant, and it had left its mark upon him. There had been the fights, and they, too, had left their marks: the white scar on his left cheek almost hidden under the dust clinging to his black stubble, the welt of a bullet on the back of his left hand.

This was Paradise Valley, this was the town of Irish Bend, remembered in the well of Morgan's memory, and yet entirely strange. Here was harbored a wickedness spawned by suspicion, a shadow across the land. It struck at Morgan from the false-fronted buildings, from the alleys, from the wide rough street. There was a sort of grim humor about it. Broad Clancy was a small man, but he threw a long wide shadow.

The tantalizing odor of cooked food brought a welling of saliva into his mouth. He had not eaten since dawn and he had been conscious of a rumbling emptiness in his stomach for hours.

Morgan turned into the hotel and immediately

31

stopped. A girl stood behind the desk and Morgan's first thought was, This is Peg. Immediately he knew he was wrong. She was small, perhaps twenty-two or three, with eager blue eyes so dark they were nearly purple. Her hair was as golden as wheat waiting for the binder, her lips were full and red and quick-smiling. No, she wasn't Peg. That gay reckless laugh had given him a picture of her, and this girl didn't fit the picture.

She motioned to an archway on his left. "That's the dining room if it's what you're looking for."

"Thanks. Just couldn't seem to get my eyes on it."

"I noticed that."

As he turned through the archway, he heard her laugh follow him, low and throaty. She wasn't, he thought, displeased.

There were a few townspeople in the dining room, two settlers with mud-caked gum boots, and one table of cowmen. The cowmen left as Morgan took a seat, and he had only a passing glance at them. One was young and small, one a thick-bodied wedge of a man, the other middle-aged and smaller than the first, with a head overlarge for his body and the conscious strut of a man who is certain of his position and power. Morgan watched him until he disappeared into the lobby. He was Broad Clancy and he fitted

32

Morgan's memory of him as perfectly as Paradise Valley had.

Morgan stepped back into the lobby when he finished dinner. He saw with keen pleasure that the girl was still at the desk. He said, "I want a room."

Nodding, she turned the register for him to sign. A pen and bottle of ink were on the desk, but he didn't write his name for a moment. To look at her was like taking a deep breath of fresh air after coming out of a tightly-closed room.

He saw things about her he had not seen before: the smooth texture of her skin, the dark tan that could have come only from long hours under the sun, the freckles on her pert nose, the perfection of her white teeth when she smiled.

She dipped the pen and handed it to him. "You have to sign your name."

"Sorry." He dropped his gaze, not realizing until then how directly he had been staring at her. "When you've been thirsty for a long time, you just can't stop drinking when you come to water."

Capping the ink bottle, she swung the register back, but she didn't look at his name for a moment. Her eyes were lifted to his and he saw no suspicion in them. Again he thought she was not displeased. She did not belong here. It was as if she stood in the sunlight away from Broad Clancy's shadow.

Then she looked down at the register as she

reached for a key. She froze that way, one hand outstretched, lips parted, and warmth fled from her face.

"Morgan. Murdo Morgan." Straightening, she gave him a direct look. "I suppose you think you're a brave man to come back."

"I never laid any claim to being a brave man," he said laconically.

"Would you admit you're a fool?"

"That'd come nearer being right."

She clutched the edge of the desk, knuckles white. "I don't think you're either one. Only the devil would return for revenge."

"If you'll give me my key, I'll find my room, ma'am. Then maybe you can tell me where Broad Clancy would be."

"Do you think I want my father's blood on my hands?" she asked hotly. "Or do you deny you returned to kill him?"

"Yes, I'll deny that. If I kill him it'll be because he forces me."

"You're a liar as well as a devil." She pointed at the black-butted gun snugging his hip. "Your brand is easy to read."

He placed his big hands palm down on the desk and leaned toward her.

"Look, Miss—"

"You were eleven when you left," she cried. "You're old enough to remember that my name is Jewell."

34

"Jewell Clancy." He said the words as if he could not believe they were her name. "I've seen desert flowers, but I didn't expect to find one here."

She blushed, but her smile did not return. "You can't stay here in the valley. Don't start the fight again."

"I don't intend to start it. I just want a room. Then I want to see your dad."

"I remember the day you left. I was in the store when you and your father rode by. I'll never forget. I've thought about it so many times. We'd killed your brothers and you'd lost your home, but you weren't crying. You were grown up, even then. Let it go at that, Murdo. All the killing you can do will not set right the wrongs we did."

"I know that," he said roughly, "and I'm tired of being called a liar. I didn't come back to kill your dad."

He saw the pulse beat in her throat, the tremor of her lips. He sensed the struggle that was in her, the desire to believe him battling what her reason told her to believe.

"Even if you are telling the truth," she whispered, "Dad won't believe you. You'll find him with Short John and Jaggers Flint in the Silver Spur. Flint's a gunman, Murdo. He'll kill you. I think Dad hired him as insurance against your return."

"Then a lot of things will be settled," he said lightly, and turned to the door.

"Don't go, Murdo," she called.

He swung back and had a long look at her. He saw her lips stir and become still; he sensed the rush of emotions that the ghost of a past not dead brought to her.

"Looks like I'll have to do without that room," he said, and left the hotel.

# Chapter 3: Clancys Are Stubborn

MURDO MORGAN WAS A DIRECT MAN WITH-
out an ounce of sly cunning in him. It was a
mark of Morgan character, just as the thin nose
and high cheekbones marked Morgan faces. He
knew that this meeting with Broad Clancy might
decide his future and the future of the valley,
and he hurried his steps as if to hasten destiny's
decision.

There were a dozen riders strung along the bar
and another group at a poker table. Turkey Track
men, Morgan guessed, for they were not squatters
and there was no other spread within fifty miles
or more of Irish Bend. If there was a fight they'd
back their boss, and that made odds which gave
Morgan no chance at all.

The Clancys and Jaggers Flint were standing
at the street end of the bar. Morgan paced slowly
to them, feeling again the covert scrutiny of every
man in the room exactly as he had felt it when he
had first ridden into town.

Broad Clancy was not over five and a half feet
tall and spindly-bodied, his face as wrinkled
as the last overripe apple in the barrel. He had
placed his expensive wide-brimmed Stetson on
the bar and his head, Murdo saw, was entirely

without hair. He turned, green eyes staring briefly at Morgan from under hooded gold-brown brows, and then coldly gave Morgan his back.

Short John, Clancy's oldest son, was about thirty the way Morgan remembered him. He was smaller than his father, but he was much like the older man, with the same green eyes and the bushy gold-brown brows. There were differences that Morgan noted; wavy brown hair worn long, muttonchop whiskers that seemed out of place on so young a man, and an intangible something that gave Morgan the impression Short John had never lived his own life, that he was forever under the shadow thrown by his father.

Short John turned his back to Morgan, making the same show of contemptuous indifference Broad had made. The slow smile that spread Morgan's mouth did not lighten the gravity of his face. He recognized this for what it was. The Clancys didn't know him, and they pretended not to care. They were the king and the crown prince; he was a stranger approaching the court. Let him bow and scrape the way other strangers did.

Anger stirred in Morgan, but he kept it masked with an urbane expression. The great pride he associated with small men was here in Broad Clancy and to a less degree in Short John.

Uncertainty had always been Morgan's lot; trouble as natural to expect as the sunset. He had been taught by the very circumstances of his life to read men. He came to the bar now and stood beside Broad Clancy, knowing that any way he played this would be a gamble, but that if he pegged Clancy right, there was one way that offered a fair chance of winning.

"You're Clancy, ain't you?" Morgan asked, his tone a cold slap at the man's dignity.

Broad Clancy stiffened. Short John turned, an audible breath sawing into the quiet. Jaggers Flint, standing beyond Short John, exploded with an oath.

"That's him, boss. That's the huckleberry who held the gun on us last night at the Smith shack."

It was the gravelly-voiced man who had been with Rip Clancy the night before. He stepped away from the bar, cocked and primed for sudden and violent trouble. Trouble was his business; he made his living that way. He was waiting to kill now, waiting only the signal from the man who had bought his gun.

According to Jewell, this was the gunman Broad Clancy had hired as insurance against Morgan's return. Morgan knew the breed. Flint had a streak that was mean and cruel, but if he was like a hundred others Morgan had known, he had another element, a weakness that would break under the pressure of hard courage. Now Morgan searched for that weakness.

"That's right, Clancy. I met up with this gent

last night. You cheated yourself when you agreed to pay him fighting wages."

Quick interest brought a bright glint in Clancy's green eyes. "Why?"

Morgan waited, letting the tension build, watching Flint's muddy brown eyes grow wide and hard and wicked, watched desire grow until it had brought him close to making a draw. He said with biting contempt: "When you pay a good price, Clancy, you deserve a good product. All you got is a phony. Just big brass buttons and an empty holler."

Desire faded in Flint's eyes. He swallowed and choked and finally said in a vain attempt to sound tough: "Nobody talks that way. Not to Jaggers Flint."

Morgan waited for the signal of his intent, the down drop of a shoulder, the tightening of his lips, the "fire glow" in his eyes. But Flint stood motionless, glowering, and Morgan prodded him with a laugh.

"Things aren't the way they used to be, Clancy. You didn't hire men like this when you cleared the valley of the Morgans."

Clancy's eyes narrowed. "What do you know about the Morgans?"

"I know quite a bit about the Morgans, but that ain't the reason I'm here. I want to talk to you. I don't take to being jumped by a gun dog. Tell him to draw or drag."

Clancy was frankly puzzled. He nodded at Flint without taking his eyes from Morgan. The gunman muttered an oath, as if reluctant to drop the matter, but he moved back to his place at the bar with greater speed than the occasion required. Morgan doubted that the man would ever have the courage to make a face-to-face draw against him, but he would be a constant threat as long as he and Morgan were both in the valley. Morgan had aroused the hate that Flint and men of his kind hold for another who has broken them. There would come a day when that hate would find expression.

"Your business?" Clancy asked in a dry, dead tone.

"I'm Murdo Morgan—"

"Morgan!" The word was jolted out of Clancy. He stood motionless, eyes twin emeralds sparking under the bushy brows, stiff-shouldered, as if the temerity of Murdo Morgan coming here had stunned him momentarily.

"I don't think you've forgotten the Morgans, Clancy."

"Murdo Morgan." Then Clancy seemed to come suddenly awake. "You came back to kill me, didn't you? Go ahead, but if you down me, you'll have a rope around your neck inside of five minutes."

"I didn't come to kill you, Clancy," Morgan said patiently. "What's been done has been done. I'm representing the—"

"I don't give a damn what you represent," Broad Clancy bawled. He jerked a thumb toward the street. "Get out. I'll give you two minutes to dust out of town."

The men at the poker tables rose and moved to the bar. More than a dozen guns. Morgan knew he could take Broad Clancy. Perhaps Short John. He couldn't take them all. But Clancy made no motion for his gun. There had been a time when he would have, but the years had slowed his draw and he had no desire to die.

"All right," Morgan said with biting scorn. "You're not as bright as I remembered you. I came here to talk over a proposition that's got to be settled before the summer's finished. There'll be lives—"

"Turkey Track stomps its own snakes," Clancy bellowed. "We make our laws and we enforce them. I've got nothing to talk over with any damned stranger, least of all a Morgan."

Short John and Jaggers Flint had moved up to stand behind Broad Clancy, the others forming a packed triangle farther along the bar. Morgan was entirely alone. A strong current ran against him, a current that would have washed a lesser man through the door and into the street.

"Forget I'm a Morgan. Put Smith or Jones or Brown or any damned handle onto me you want to. If you'll listen you might be able to save Turkey Track. If you don't—"

"You've used up your time," Clancy said coldly. "Ride out of the valley."

Morgan had forgotten the barkeep. If he were shot in the back, there would be no avenging justice. Only a quick burial. They'd plant him below the east rim beside the three Morgans who had lain there for sixteen years. He backed along the bar until he could see the apron. Straightening, the man laid a shotgun on the mahogany, face a frozen mask.

Morgan's smile was a cold straight line toughening his bronze face. He said: "You used to be a fighting man, Clancy, but you're old and you're tired, so you hire punks like Flint and wink at a barman to shoot a man in the back. I'm not here to argue. I came to stop a fight, but if fight is what you want, it's fight you'll get."

Morgan backed out of the Silver Spur and slanted across the intersection formed by Main and the side street. He paced along the front of the Elite saloon and on past two empty buildings, moving with challenging slowness.

Stepping into the livery stable, Morgan paid the hostler and got his black, ignoring the open malice on the man's face. Mounting, he rode across the street, stepped down in front of the post office and tied his mount. A hasty departure from town would mean that he had been stampeded by Broad Clancy, an advantage he could not afford to give the cowman.

Morgan paused in front of the post office, shaping a smoke and lighting it, eyes on the pine-fringed slopes of the Sunset Mountains. A cloud bank lay above the pines, slowly building into strange grotesque shapes. When he had finished, he tossed his cigarette into the street and turned into the post office. He bought a card from the white-haired postmistress, scratched a note to Grant Gardner in San Francisco, and mailed it.

"Murdo."

It was Jewell Clancy's voice. He wheeled back to the wicket. The girl was standing where the old lady had been a moment before, her gaze speculative and interested.

"Do the Clancys run the post office along with everything else in the valley?" he asked.

"This is the only place where I could talk to you without Dad seeing me. When I saw you come in, I ran around to the back."

"I had a notion you didn't want to talk to me."

Still her gaze was held on him, as if trying to cut away the real motives that had driven him back after all the years. He saw no fear of him in her eyes, no bitterness, no hatred.

She was grave, not even a hint of a smile lingering at the corners of her lips. "I was outside the Silver Spur and heard what you said. I . . . I was wrong about you. You didn't come back to kill Dad."

"I didn't expect to hear such confidence from a Clancy."

"Why did you come, Murdo?"

He took off his hat in a quick gesture, as if suddenly remembering it was on his head, a gesture of gallantry that surprised and pleased her. He held his silence for a time, pondering her reason for asking. Perhaps Broad Clancy, regretting he had not listened, had sent Jewell to find out his mission. He said finally, "I'll tell your dad when he's of a mind to listen."

"They say all Clancys are stubborn," she said, "but Dad is the stubbornest of all of us. If he wasn't he'd have seen what I did. When you backed Flint down, you could have forced a fight on Dad and killed him. That's how I knew I was wrong."

"If I'd come here to do a killing job," Morgan murmured, "I wouldn't have used the Morgan name."

"I thought of that, too." Her smile brought back a little of the warmth he had first seen on her face. "You see, I'm almost as much of a lost soul as you are. Dad can't understand how a Clancy can see two sides to the trouble."

"Can you?"

"Yes. It wasn't all Dad's fault. Or did you know that?"

"No."

"I'll tell you about it sometime. It isn't impor-

45

tant now. If you aren't here to kill Dad, you're here for another reason. If I knew what it was, I could help you."

"No, you can't help."

"Dad will keep on thinking you're here to kill him," she urged, "so he'll try to kill you first."

"I reckon he'll try."

"Auntie Jones is the postmistress. If you want me, get word to her."

"Thanks."

Morgan left the post office, pausing again outside to build a smoke. He was still there when Jewell came through the doorway behind him and walked gracefully across the street, a hand lifting her skirt from trim ankles as she waded the dust.

# Chapter 4: The Girl Peg

THE AFTERNOON SUN PRESSED AGAINST Morgan's back as he took the east road out of town. The miles fell behind, miles that were monotonously alike: flat, sandy earth, sage and rabbit brush, an occasional juniper that seemed to huddle within itself as it struggled to hold the small moisture its roots sucked from the arid land.

Then Morgan topped a ridge and came down to Paradise Lake. It was no thing of beauty. Tules grew profusely in the muck along the west end of the lake. A long-snouted hog, suddenly aware of his presence, snorted defiance and crashed into the swamp growth.

On the north side of the lake the alkali flat, entirely without life, shimmered in the sharp brightness of the sunshine. It was worthless, but the south side of the lake was the most valuable part of the valley. Here were thousands of acres that could be farmed without water, for it would always be moist from the lake. Pete Royce's place, the only farm in this part of the valley, took up but a small fraction of the rich black soil that stretched to the south.

The road skirted the front of Royce's farm. A

47

brown haystack from the previous year bulked wide in the field between the road and the lake; around it grass bowed in long rhythmical waves before the hot wind that had sprung up. Southward, gray desert stretched in sage-studded ridges toward the buttes.

Presently Morgan came to Royce's cabin. It was made, he guessed, of lodgepole pine brought from Clancy Mountain. There was a scattering of sheds and corrals, and what was most surprising, a well kept lawn between the cabin and the road. Even without the obvious evidence of the washing on the line, Morgan would have guessed a woman lived here.

Dismounting, Morgan watered his horse at the trough. A saddled bay gelding was racked at the hitch pole in front of the cabin. The door was open, and as Morgan turned to step back into the saddle, he heard a laugh, gay and entirely feminine. With a sudden sharpening of interest, Morgan realized that the girl Peg was inside.

Morgan would have ridden on if he hadn't heard the girl ask, "What are you going to do about the company man when he shows up, Rip?"

"I'll fill him so full of lead he won't float in the lake. It'll take more'n a company gunslinger to run us Clancys off our range." Stepping around the trough, Morgan walked up the path that cut across the lawn. Something was wrong. No one but Ed Cole and Gardner and his organization knew that Morgan was coming to Paradise Valley.

Morgan paused in the doorway, an angular shape nearly filling it, right hand idle at his side. He said coldly: "I'm the company man you were expecting, Clancy. Now what was it you were going to do?"

Young Clancy and the girl were sitting on a leather sofa pushed against the north wall. Grabbing his gun, Clancy came up from his seat as if a giant spring had shot him upright. Then he froze, color washing out of his scrawny-thin face. He was looking into the black bore of Morgan's gun.

"You're hell with the talk," Morgan said contemptuously, "but a mite slow on the draw."

Morgan would have recognized Rip as a Clancy. He had the same arrogance and exaggerated pride, the green eyes and the bushy brows, but they were red, not gold-brown, and his hair was red. He straightened, slender hands moving nervously as he sought a way out of this.

"I know your voice," Rip cried. "You're the hombre who covered up for Buck last night."

"That's right."

"I should of plugged you," Rip said regretfully. "Flint talked me out of it. I didn't think he was that short of guts."

"A Clancy wouldn't be short of guts, would he? Want me to put my iron back and give you another chance to draw?"

Rip ran the tip of his tongue over dry lips. He

49

shot a glance at the girl, sharp features growing sharper as hate pressed him, as the humiliation of this moment cut deeper into his pride.

Morgan let the tension build until Rip flung out, "You've got the edge now, mister. Go ahead and walk big. There'll be another day."

"I'll wait for it, sonny."

Morgan remained in the doorway, gun hip-high, watching young Clancy narrowly. He sensed a cold courage in the boy that had been lacking in Broad and Short John. As he watched, a wicked grin broke across Rip's narrow face.

Without turning, Morgan knew he had made a mistake. He had seen only the one horse, and it had not occurred to him that Rip would have another man with him. Now, from the mocking triumph in the boy's eyes, he knew someone was behind him.

There was no time to think about it, to let it play out. He whirled with the unexpectedness and speed of a striking cougar, his gun lashing out with a ribbon of flame. A bullet burned along Morgan's ribs, but the man in the yard didn't fire again. Morgan had moved with perfect coordination of instinct and muscular speed. His bullet had knocked the man off his feet as if he'd been sledged by an ax handle.

Time had compressed and run out for Murdo Morgan. Rip Clancy was behind him with a gun on his hip and all the opportunity he needed.

Morgan spun back. Then he held his fire. The girl had gripped Clancy's wrist. She was screaming, "No, Rip! No!"

Morgan reached Clancy in two long strides. "I'll take that cutter. I didn't think the Clancys would whipsaw a man like that."

"The man you shot wasn't a Clancy," Peg said without feeling. "He's Pete Royce."

Clancy stood perfectly still as Morgan took his gun, shoulder blades pressed against the wall. His face was bone-hard, eyes frosty slits. "What kind of a woman are you, Peg?" he demanded hoarsely. "I'd have plugged him if you—"

"I know you would have," the girl breathed, "and I've got an idea about any crawling thing that would shoot a man in the back."

Red crept into Clancy's cheeks as he felt the girl's scorn. He held his position, saying nothing. Morgan holstered his gun and kneeling beside the man in the yard, saw that the bullet had creased his skull. It was a shallow wound, enough to knock him cold but unlikely to prove dangerous. Morgan lifted him and carried him into the cabin.

"Got a sawbones in town?" Morgan asked.

"Doc Velie. Go fetch him, Rip."

Young Clancy didn't move for a moment, sullen green eyes whipping from Peg to Morgan and back to Peg. He had been beaten; he had taken the girl's contempt, and pride had been torn from him and trampled underfoot.

"All right," Clancy muttered. "Don't figger I'm done with you, mister; and I've got an idea that when Pete gets up and finds out what you done, he'll take a blacksnake to you, Peg."

"I'll kill him if he does," the girl said. "He'll never beat me again."

"Big wind blowing off the lake," Clancy jeered. "He'll curry you down like he's done before. Or mebbe I'll do it myself. You've had your fun playing with me and Buck Carrick. One of these days I'll have some fun of my own."

Clancy stalked out, hit saddle, and went down the road at a hard run, cracking steel to his horse every jump.

Morgan watched while Peg washed the crimson trickle from Pete Royce's face and stopped the flow of blood with a bandage.

"Sorry I had to shoot him," Morgan murmured.

"You've got no call to be sorry." She rose and faced him. "I wouldn't have been sorry if you'd shot him between the eyes."

"He's your father?"

"So he says. If he is, I'm not proud of my blood."

Morgan built a smoke, standing lax, back against the wall. This was the first opportunity he'd had to appraise the girl, and he took his time with his cigarette, head bent a little, eyes fixed on her.

Peg Royce was tall with dark eyes and cricket-

black hair combed sleekly back from her forehead and tied with a bright red ribbon. She was
eighteen or twenty, Morgan guessed, with a
woman's full-bodied roundness. She stood beside
the couch, ramrod-straight, making her study of
him as coolly as he studied her. She came toward
him then, moving in a graceful leggy stride.

"You're a fighting man," she said. "I felt it last
night, and I had proof just now. You're worth any
three men in the valley, but that isn't enough. The
company should have sent an army."

She was standing close to him, head tilted, the
fragrance of her hair a stirring sweetness in his
nostrils, red lips invitingly close. He saw the
pulse beat in her white throat, felt the pressure of
her high pointed breasts. She set up a turbulence
in him, speeded his heart until it was pounding
with hammerlike beats in his chest.

"I've done all right," he said. "With your help."

"I won't always be around. If the Clancy outfit
doesn't get you, Dad or some of the other nesters
will. You won't live the week out."

"I never gamble with anybody's life but my
own." He slid past her into the yard. "Keep your
dad quiet till the doc gets here. Head wounds are
pretty tricky."

"Nobody keeps Pete Royce quiet," she said
with sharp bitterness.

"Why do you hate him?"

"Because of what he's done and what he will

53

do. You'll hate him when you know him. You're here to get him off company land, aren't you?" She shook her head. "He won't go and he won't pay for the land. Go in there and put a bullet through his head. You'll never get him off any other way."

She remained in the doorway, scowling against the sun. Looking at her now, Morgan saw the lines of discontent that cut her forehead. Suddenly she put it away. She laughed, as gay and free a laugh as she had given Buck Carrick the night before.

"You wouldn't kill him when he couldn't fight back, would you? You're that kind of a fool. The trouble is Pete Royce and Arch Blazer and the Clancys don't play by rule."

"You're pretty as an angel," he said in a puzzled voice, "and as tough as a bootheel."

"That's me." She came across the yard to him. "Nobody knows what I am. Maybe I don't know myself, but I've learned a little about playing this game that every woman has played since Eve had her fun. I'll use a man to get what I want, and I'll have a winner when the last hand's played. A lot of pious people like the Clancys say I'm bad, but I'm honest, and that's more than you can say for them."

"Do you call it honest to play a man against another until one of them is dead because of you?"

"Who's dead?"

"Buck Carrick might have been after you put Rip onto his tail last night."

"I didn't do anything of the kind. Murdo Morgan, don't make me worse than I am."

"Then why did Rip come to the shack after Buck?"

"I'd met Buck there before. Old man Carrick hates me. That's why we meet at the shack. Rip probably saw me ride across the valley."

"How did you know my name and that I'm a company man?"

"The wind talks," she said lightly, "and I understand it. I saw you watering your horse, so I started talking to Rip about the company man. We don't have many strangers here. I just made a good guess who you were."

"You wanted me to come in?"

"Sure. I wanted to see a fight. You know. Get a man killed over me."

He had called it right. She was as tough as a bootheel. There was little shame or modesty about her. She'd use a man to get what she wanted exactly as she'd said. Suddenly he was angry. There was no good reason for it except that he resented her coolly confident smile, her frank assurance that she could have him and use him exactly as she had Rip Clancy and Buck Carrick.

"Thanks for keeping Clancy off my back."

"Don't thank me. I wanted you alive."

Morgan stepped into the saddle. He sat looking down at her, knowing he had no reason to stay, but not wanting to go. He said, "Tell Royce I want to talk to him when he gets on his feet."

"He'll never talk to a company man. He'll work around so you'll get killed and nobody will know he had a hand in it. But you're too big a fool to ride out of the country. You'll stay and you'll come back here." She stood with her legs widespread, red lips forming a cool smile, a graceful, seductively-shaped figure. "You'll be back, but not to see Pete Royce, and I'll go on trying to keep you alive."

He turned his horse into the road. He didn't look back, but he knew she was standing there, staring at him and perhaps smiling. She would be a dangerous enemy, or a friend who could never be fully trusted.

Nature had endowed Peg Royce with all the weapons in the feminine arsenal and taught her their use. He knew how to fight men like Jaggers Flint and Rip Clancy, how and when to push. He didn't know how to fight Peg Royce. He tried to put her out of his mind, but she clung there tenaciously, disturbing him, and whipping his pulse to a faster pace.

Buck Carrick had said: "Don't ever see her. She'll drag you through hell. She's poison." Now Morgan knew what Buck had meant, but the knowledge made no difference. She remained in his mind.

When Morgan was out of sight, Peg turned back into the cabin, a grave soberness coming into her face. For a long time she stared down at Pete Royce, bitterness and frustration flooding her consciousness.

"You've sold your soul to Ed Cole for $1,000, Royce," she whispered. "You'll kill the best man who ever rode into the valley, but you can't have my soul to take to hell with you. Not for all your $1,000."

# Chapter 5: Born a Clancy

WATCHING THE STREET FROM HER HOTEL window, Jewell Clancy saw Murdo Morgan leave town. She remembered his father Josh. She remembered the older Morgan boys less distinctly, but the years had not blurred the clear picture her memory held of the boy Murdo as he had ridden through town beside his father.

Perhaps it was the contrast between Murdo and his father that had blazed the picture so deeply in her mind. Josh Morgan had been a beaten man. All the things he had lived for, the things he had loved, were gone. Broad Clancy had exacted his revenge. There had been nothing left for Josh but sad memories, an ideal, and the eleven-year-old boy beside him. Murdo had had no trace of that whipped-dog look. Thinking about it now, she saw again his tight-lipped face, the eyes without tears that stared straight ahead. In her heart she must have known all these years that Murdo Morgan would come back.

Even as a child she had sensed the hate her father held for the Morgans. She did not understand what caused it, but she listened to the war talk; she had felt the corrosive effect of that hate. She remembered her father bringing her and

Rip, no more than a baby then, into town; she remembered the heavily armed cavalcade that had swept eastward. Short John, little older than Murdo, had gone with the men.

She remembered the hushed stillness that lay upon the tiny town. If the Morgans won, someone said, Irish Bend would be burned to the ground. But they couldn't win. The odds were too great. Still, fear had gripped the townspeople, for Josh Morgan and his sons were respected as fighting men.

She remembered the firing, close at first, then dying. Hours later her father rode back into town at the head of his men. Short John beside him, trying to look as tough and proud as Broad had told him a Clancy should look, and failing. It was something Short John had always failed at, but something Rip did very well.

Watching Morgan's tall square-shouldered back until he disappeared, she wondered how it would have gone in the Silver Spur if Rip had been with her father and Short John. It would, she knew, have been a fight, but she could not guess how it would have turned out. If she had judged Murdo Morgan right, he would have had a chance even against the kind of odds he faced in the saloon.

She moved from the window, dissatisfaction breeding a restlessness in her, and paused for a moment in front of the mirror. She found no fault with her appearance, small-bodied and full-lipped, with wheat-gold hair that never stayed pinned up the way she wanted it. Quickly she turned away, took her embroidery from a bureau drawer and sat down to work on it. The restlessness grew in her. She had no desire to grow old without husband or children or her own home, but none of the eligible men in the valley gave her a passing glance. The reason she knew, was the fact that she was a Clancy. If a man did show interest, Broad changed his mind.

She forced herself to stay with her self-given task, her thoughts continually turning to Morgan. His appearance had stirred alive the memories and thoughts she had tried to submerge in her mind. She was a Clancy. Nothing could change that, not even the hate she felt for the things her father had done and the things he would do. His arbitrary rule of the valley, his possession of a range that did not belong to him, his battering down of the pride and self-respect of the settlers and townsmen.

She knew nothing of the outside world except what she heard from drummers who stopped at the hotel, but she knew everything about her immediate world, for she spent more time riding than she did at home or in the hotel. She was never sure in her own mind why she rode so much, except that she had to get away from the empire Broad Clancy had built and ruled.

Hate was always there, oppressive and weighty.

Intolerance. Pride bordering on arrogance that prompted Broad to tell and retell the story of the Morgan defeat. Decisions that regulated others and should have been made by them. Everything in her rebelled against the atmosphere that was constant in the big ranchhouse. There were two escapes: a horse with the wild wind against her face, and Irish Bend.

The hotel belonged to her. It had been Broad's idea. Turkey Track was not for a woman. It would be Short John's and Rip's, but she had to have some way of making a living, so Broad had given her the hotel.

"You've got to know the business," Broad had often told her. "Same as Short John and Rip have got to know cattle. This will always be a good stock country and there'll always be a town here. If you run it right, your hotel will fetch you a good living."

So she had set out to learn the business, taking her turn at the desk or helping out in the kitchen and dining room.

Broad had furnished this room for her. Perhaps it had been a way of proving his affection. Or perhaps, and this was more likely, he wanted to let the town know that a Clancy could afford something better than anyone else. Whatever his motive, he had furnished it well. It was a sort of combination bedroom and parlor with walnut furniture, a thick carpet that deadened the heaviest footfall, an orange velvet-covered love seat, and Battenberg lace curtains at the windows.

Broad had not asked Jewell what she wanted for her room. He had gone to Portland and ordered the furnishings and had them freighted to Irish Bend. It was hers whether she liked it or not. She had thanked him and pretended everything was what she wanted. Under other circumstances she would have liked everything in the room. It was that the furnishings had not been of her choosing, that he had not asked her. It was, in itself, typical of everything in her life.

There was one thing about staying at the hotel that she liked. She could visit with people who were not directly under Broad Clancy's thumb: Auntie Jones, who could talk of woman things that Jewell could not talk about in a man-ruled ranchhouse; Doc Velie, the one person in the valley who was not afraid of Broad Clancy, crusty and independent and filled with knowledge and sympathy for others; Abel Purdy, who must have read, Jewell thought, every book that had ever been printed. He bowed to Broad so he could hold his jobs, for he was town marshal, mayor, and justice of the peace, and Clancy saw to it that Irish Bend was attentive to Turkey Track interest.

She rose and put her embroidery away, still finding no answer to the question that had been nagging her mind all afternoon. "If Morgan had not returned for revenge, what had brought him back?" But he had returned, a fact big enough in itself to promise violent changes in what had been an even way of life.

She combed out her hair and put it up again for want of something better to do. Even in the few minutes she had talked to Morgan, she had seen things in him she liked. If any man had reason to go bad, it was Murdo Morgan, but he had not. She was as sure of that as she was sure of any pattern of human behaviour.

She had misjudged him at first and she had tried to make up for it in the post office. She was not sure he had believed her. She thought, with a sudden spasm of alarm, that she might never have another chance to convince him she wanted to help him.

Finished with her hair, she returned to the desk in the lobby. Without conscious direction, her thoughts turned to Abel Purdy, who knew so much and was so unhappy. He had said once: "You live in your own small hell, but you're still the happiest woman I know. You always look as if you were anticipating something good and were eager for it, and you're hiding a smile in the corners of your mouth even when you're grave."

It was the nicest thing anyone had ever said to her, and she cherished it. Doc Velie would say nice things, but always with a crusty note that took the edge off. Doc was as likely as not to call

Broad Clancy a two-legged hog using land for cows that five thousand people could live on, and Broad would cuss Doc for saying it. Still, and this was something Jewell did not understand, Broad had more respect for Doc Velie than he did for Abel Purdy who never crossed him.

Jewell was still at the desk when Rip rode into town, called to Doc Velie and racked his horse in front of the Silver Spur. A minute later Velie left town and Jewell knew Rip had come for him. Anxiety struck at her. Morgan had gone that way. Rip might have met and killed him. Then she put the thought away. Murdo Morgan had the look of a man who would take a lot of killing.

Presently Broad left the saloon, Short John on one side of him, Rip on the other. They crossed the street to the hotel, came to the desk, and without a word, Broad spun the register and looked at it. "Murdo Morgan." He lifted green eyes to Jewell's face. "He signed his name. Why didn't he stay?"

"I was a little rough with him. I thought he had come back to kill you."

"You were rough?" Rip laughed. "I'm the one who is gonna get rough. The next time I see him—"

"You'll fight him fair," Broad said sharply. "A Clancy doesn't have to shoot a man in the back. You can thank the Royce girl for keeping you from committing murder."

"We've got a reputation," Short John put in. "Don't forget you're a Clancy."

Jewell felt pity for her older brother. That was the way he always was, trying to live up to what Broad expected from him and succeeding no better than an echo succeeds in outdoing its source.

Rip wheeled on Short John. "Keep your lip buttoned," he said with cold fury. "I'll be damned if I'll take a rawhiding from you."

Short John drew back, offended. "All right, all right. Hell, I didn't ask to be born a Clancy, but I was, and I'll try to act like one."

"You might remember that, too, Jewell," Broad said.

For the first time she realized he had been staring at her. Puzzled, she asked, "Why did you say that?"

"You went to the post office when Morgan was there. Why?"

"To talk to him," she said angrily. "I know what happened in the Silver Spur, and I can't see that it would have been any different for Rip to shoot a man in the back than for you to have a barkeep do it."

Fury roared in Broad Clancy. The meeting with Morgan had left a scar upon him. It would be a goading memory as long as he lived. Now his bushy brows flattened above his eyes; his weather-beaten face went tight with the rush of passion. For a moment she thought he was going to strike her. Then, regaining control of himself, he laid his hands palm down on the desk top. "If you were a boy—"

"You've never understood the difference," she cut in.

He swallowed. "Damn the day the Lord made women."

She turned to Rip, ignoring Broad. "Who was hurt?"

"Pete Royce. I was visiting Peg when Morgan showed up. He drilled Royce."

It was probably only part of the truth, but she would get the rest from Doc Velie. She asked, "Why is Morgan here?"

"Company man," Rip grunted. "Either we get him or we don't have no spread."

Jewell turned her gaze to her father. "You've known this was coming. You could have bought enough company land to have held—"

"Morgan can go to hell," Broad cried. "If he's got as much savvy as his old man, he'll slope out of the country. If he stays, we'll get him when the sign's right. I don't want no talk out of you about buying from the company as long as Morgan's hooked up with it and I don't want to hear none of Doc Velie's gab coming out of you about using good farm land for cow pasture."

It came to her for the first time that Broad Clancy had lost some of the hard-driving courage he had once possessed. He would not have talked, even a few years ago, about waiting for the sign to be right. The years had dulled the fine edge from his ruthless energy. They had brought no softness to him, but he had changed. For years he had lived by the reputation he had made. Now that Morgan had called his hand, Broad would handle him in a safe roundabout way.

"I don't want to see you lose Turkey Track," she said.

"I won't lose it," he bellowed as if the sound of his own voice gave him confidence. "You don't need to be wasting your sympathy. Waste it on Morgan. I'll settle with the company when I get good and ready, and not till Morgan's been taken care of." He chewed a thin lip, head lowered like a runty bull, gaze pushing at Jewell. "And it'll be fair, damn you." He swung to Rip. "Another thing. Quit seeing that Royce hussy. I'll have no half-nester brats running around Turkey Track."

"Why," Rip said lightly, "a man's got a right to his fun. A Clancy man anyway."

Jewell understood the lewd glance that passed between them. It was the thing she hated most in her father and brothers. A woman was good for only one purpose. As far as she, Broad's daughter, was concerned, she could run the hotel and be an old maid.

"O.K., son, if that's the way it is." Broad wheeled to the door. "Let's dust."

A moment later the Clancy men rode out of town toward the west, Turkey Track buckaroos a long line behind them. Jewell watched them go, a thousand mixed-up feelings in her heart. She was afraid to look ahead, but the pressure of what was bound to come pushed at her. Time had caught up with the Clancys and with the valley. Nothing would be quite the same again. If it wasn't Murdo Morgan, it would be someone else, yet there had been a time when Broad Clancy could have bought the company land for close to his own price. Perhaps it was not yet too late, but she knew him too well to think that he would make any effort as long as Morgan represented the company.

There was no smile lingering in the corners of her mouth now, no hint of eagerness about her. Staring at the gray dust rising behind the riders, she whispered, "Must the Clancys always live upon the meat and bones of other men?"

# Chapter 6: The Carricks

THE ROAD BEYOND THE ROYCE PLACE WAS no more than two vague ruts cut through the sage. As Morgan followed it, a thousand memories crowded back into a mind already too full. He thought again of his boyhood; the long trip north from California with the herd, his hound dog Tuck, the clean sharp sound of ax on pine as his father and brothers built the cabin, the first deer he'd shot. He remembered his father's words, "There's room enough for us and the Clancys in this valley. Some day the settlers will come, and we'll help them when they do, but right now we'll take what we can hold."

But there had not been enough room in the valley and the Morgans had been unable to hold a square foot. Morgan never knew what had started the fight, but it had been destined from the first. Broad Clancy and Josh Morgan had known each other years before, and the capacity for hatred was great in both of them. Clancy had won because he had been the first in the valley, and with his greater wealth, he had been able to hire more men.

Morgan swung north from the road and presently reached the rimrock which made a twenty-foot cliff at his place. A short distance to the north a creek spilled over the edge in a crystal waterfall. Here the three Morgan boys were buried, close to the creek they had loved and on a ridge from which Murdo, looking westward, could see the great sweep of the valley.

Morgan idled there for a time, surprised by the way the graves had been kept. The grass was green and trimmed, the fence was as tight as Josh had left it, and the headstones were in place. The Carricks must have taken care of the little cemetery, and that puzzled him.

More memories. Poignant. Heart-deep. Memories he had not known were there. The last fight. Broad Clancy had used every cowhand he had and all the gunmen he could hire. He had made the attack with the deadly intention of rubbing out the Morgans.

Murdo had been told to stay at home. Only his father had come back, wounded, face gray with disappointment and pain and heartache. He was done fighting. He had taken the shotgun away from Murdo, who had been only eleven and filled with fury and hate when he heard what had happened. He remembered crying, "I can't miss Broad with buckshot. Lemme have it."

But Josh had shaken his head. "It's over. We'd be gone now if we didn't have to wait for the funeral. We've got to dig the graves."

Murdo Morgan had helped dig the graves.

Some of the townsmen had brought the boys home. Stiff and bloody, these brothers he had walked and ridden and hunted with. But they were not his brothers then. Just bodies. The hollow sound of clods on the pine coffins. His father's frozen face. The preacher who had come from Prineville. He had looked across the open graves at Broad Clancy and talked about the boys who had been cut down in the bloom of their youth, and Clancy had stared back boldly.

Morgan had never understood why Clancy had come to the funeral. It hadn't seemed right. Clancy or his men had killed his brothers and then had come to see them buried. Morgan had cried after the funeral. He had run into the cabin to hunt for the shotgun and when he couldn't find it, he had dropped on the bed and cried. He had never cried before like that nor had he since.

They had left that afternoon, Josh Morgan and Murdo, taking a pack horse and a few of the things Josh wanted as keepsakes, one of them a tintype of Murdo's mother. That last look at the valley, the smoke plume rising from the burning cabin. Those were things a man would never forget if he lived as long as the desert had been here. Nor could he forget his father's words: "There's room for a thousand families down there where Broad Clancy runs his cattle. I'm going to bring them and I'll bust Clancy. That ain't important, but giving homes to hungry people is."

But Josh Morgan had died too soon. This was another day and it was Murdo Morgan and not Josh who stood here. Breaking Broad Clancy was less important to Murdo than it had been to his father. He had seen Clancy today. He was not the terror Morgan had remembered. He was an old man, tormented by more fear than he would ever admit, a rich man trying to hold to something that had never been his, and Morgan was glad he had not found the shotgun that day of the funeral. Clancy had not changed his ways, but time had brought its punishment and it would bring more.

Turning from the graves, Morgan mounted and rode toward the Carrick cabin. It had been built on the ashes of the bigger Morgan house. The row of poplars Josh had planted had been little more than switches when Morgan had left. Now they were tall slender trees, throwing a shade laced with golden sunlight across the yard.

A huge fireplace centered the lodgepole pine cabin. It winked brightly from a thousand eyes as Morgan rode up. When he was close, he saw that broken pieces of obsidian had been set among the other rocks. Lilac bushes grew at the end of the cabin, their blossoms spreading a haunting fragrance around them. It was a pleasant place, more pleasant than Morgan remembered.

Emotions, long suppressed by the simplicity of his life, rose uninhibited.

Two men were idling at the corral, a saddled horse standing behind them. They had been watching Morgan's approach, and now the dark-bearded one raised a hand in greeting, and called amiably, "Light, stranger."

Pulling up beside them, Morgan stepped down and held out his hand. "I'm guessing you're Jim Carrick."

"That's a plumb good guess," the bearded man boomed. He motioned to the slender man at his side. "My boy, Tom."

"I'm Murdo Morgan." He shook young Carrick's hand and quickly dropped it. It was damp and withdrawing as the man himself was withdrawing.

"Morgan," Jim Carrick cried. "You ain't kin to them three we got buried over yonder?"

"Brother."

"You remember when it happened, don't you?" Tom demanded eagerly. "You came back to fight 'em, didn't you?"

"What's done is done. If it's a fight, Broad Clancy will make it."

Disgust stirred Tom's leathery face. "Hell, what kind of man are you, toting a gun thataway and talking like a pan of milk." He spat a brown ribbon into the dust that stirred it briefly. "Bluejohn milk at that."

"Enough gab," Jim Carrick said sharply. "You don't need to look for a fight all the time."

Young Carrick cursed bitterly. His was a barren, vindictive face. He wore a bushy mustache that was tobacco-stained and his clothes were a cowman's, not a nester's. His bone-handled Colt was carried low and thonged down in the manner of a man who fights for pay. He was not one to be found on a nester place, and Morgan, watching him closely, was puzzled by him.

Tom ran the back of his hand along his mouth. "If I had three brothers salivated like them Morgan boys was and I came back after all this time, I wouldn't look for no fight. I'd sure as hell get out and make one." Wheeling, he mounted and lined south along the rimrock.

"Mighty proddy, Tom is," Jim Carrick said worriedly. "He don't take to being pushed around by the Clancys. I don't, neither, but I don't see no way of living on this range if you don't stand for being pushed some."

Jim Carrick was as big a man as Morgan, with brown eyes that were both friendly and honest, and dark hair holding no more gray than the bushy beard. He pulled a pipe from his pocket and dribbled tobacco into it, great hands trembling with the bottled-up emotion that was in him.

"A man can stand only so much pushing," Morgan said.

"Yeah." Carrick slid the tobacco pouch back into his pocket. "I heard that old man Morgan died after Clancy ran him out of the valley, but I didn't know he had a kid." He swung a big hand away from him in an all-inclusive gesture. "Enough graze for two big outfits. No sense of Clancy trying to be both God and the devil. Being the devil is enough for one man."

"A cowman's paradise," Morgan murmured. "Mild winters, plenty of bunchgrass, and good summer graze plumb over to Harney County. Dad used to say that."

Carrick scratched a match on the top corral bar and fired his pipe. Between puffs he said: "That's right. I reckon Broad Clancy's made more money that he can count. Don't cost much to raise beef 'cause his grass is free for the taking. The herd he hazes south to the railroad in Californy makes the cattle they raise down there look downright puny. Don't get the diseases up here they do in the warmer climates."

"Dad used to say that the cowmen pioneered the way into a new country, but the farmers always came later. He said that in the long run stockmen couldn't hold a million acres to support maybe a hundred men, while a thousand families could make a good living on the same amount of land if it was taken care of."

"Your dad was sure as hell right. So's Teddy Roosevelt, near as I can see. Damned good

President. Got some of those same ideas. It's time somebody was stepping in and looking after the grass. Clancy ain't overgrazed this valley, but I've seen plenty of places the cowmen have." Carrick shrugged and motioned toward the green strip marking the creek. "That ain't the point here. This is a case of one man being too big for his britches."

"Clancy don't own the valley."

"Might as well. There ain't a dozen of us farmer families in the valley. We live where Clancy tells us and we live the way he tells us or we've got trouble. Why, a man can raise mighty near anything. Reckon it could be a fruit country, but that's just crazy dreaming."

"One of these times Clancy will stump his toe."

Carrick laughed sourly. "Looks to me like he's walking mighty good. I ain't proddy like Tom, but I'm about ready to fight or quit calling myself a man. When you said you was a Morgan, I was hoping you aimed to throw some lead Clancy's way."

"What are the rest of the nesters like?"

"Pete Royce is a double-crossing coyote who'd slit your throat for a nickel. Arch Blazer is a barroom fighter and meaner'n Royce. They're the worst. Some of the others are hiding out, I reckon, thinking the law will never find 'em out here. The rest are like sheep, hating Clancy but kotowing to him all the same."

"By fall you'll see a thousand families living here," Morgan said. "Then Broad Clancy will sing a new tune."

Carrick took his sweat-stained hat from his head and ran a hand over his face. "If it wasn't so damned hot, I'd laugh. What makes you think there'll be a thousand families in here by fall?"

"The Cascade & Paradise Land Company is selling acreage in the Middle West now. After the drought and the grasshoppers they've had, they'll be of a mind to buy and try it out here."

"So the land company is finally gonna do it," Carrick murmured. "I'd heard the old bunch had sold out. Pull your gear off your horse, Morgan. I'll go rustle a drink."

Jim Carrick would do. Morgan offsaddled, turned his black into the corral, and swung toward the cabin. He had to have help, and Carrick was a better man than he could rightfully expect to find. Usually men who stood for the kind of pushing that Clancy gave were, as Carrick had hinted, men who would accept anything in exchange for a place where they could live without fear of the law catching up with them.

Carrick waited in the shade of the poplars until Morgan caught up and led the way into the cabin. "Ain't the kind of place your dad built, I reckon, but we make out."

There was one long room, the cavernous fireplace built into the south wall, a stove and table and chairs at one end with shelves above the stove for the pots and pans and food. There were bunks at the other end, the blankets neatly made up. Clothes hung from pegs driven into the north wall, the puncheon floor was as clean as sweeping could make it, and there was none of the usual litter that Morgan had come to expect in a womanless household.

Carrick found a bottle on a shelf and turning, paused when he saw Morgan looking up at a woman's picture on the wall. She was a young woman, slim-faced, with small exact features. The frame was bronze and carved into too many extravagant curlicues, a wrong kind of frame, Morgan thought, for a face that pretty. He turned to see Carrick watching him intently.

"My wife," Carrick said. "Tom takes after her."

"A fine-looking woman," Morgan said.

"She was." Carrick's face had gone entirely sober. "We tried it up north around Hampton Butte, but it was too tough. When we got down here, she was sick. Never got up. Clancy came the day we finished the cabin and told us how we'd live. Had about ten men with him and he talked mighty damned tough. Tom was gonna pull on him. Mamma, she stopped the trouble, but it was too much for her. She died the next week, and I've been having a hell of a time holding Tom down since then."

"Another score to settle with Clancy," Morgan

said. "I didn't thank you for keeping the graves up."

"No need to thank me. I didn't know nothing about the Morgans. I just knew they'd died fighting the Clancys, and I figured that if the day ever came when there was enough of us to fight, it'd do everybody good to know that other men had cashed in for the same reason. Them graves stand for something. That was why we buried Mamma in town. I saved the spot for your brothers."

"Thanks anyhow," Morgan said. "I wasn't around to keep them up. If you hadn't, I couldn't have found them for the weeds."

"I've got a notion that sometime, maybe not on this earth, but somewhere, that a man like Broad Clancy is gonna get taken care of. It's just the way I've got the Lord figgered." He stepped through the door. "Come on. It's cooler out here."

Morgan followed Carrick to the patch of shade and sat down in the battered leather chair Carrick indicated. "It's hot as hell for this early."

Carrick handed him the bottle. "This'll make you forget it. Makes me forget most everything but Broad Clancy. Now let's hear you talk. If the land company is what I think it is, you won't get more'n one drink outta that bottle."

Morgan grinned as he took the bottle. "Hard choice between Clancy and the land company, ain't it?"

"Damned hard." Carrick dropped to the ground and put his back to a poplar trunk. "There just ain't enough of us to fight either one. You can't count on men like Royce and Blazer."

"The law's on the company's side," Morgan said quietly.

"That's the hell of it. All of us, including Clancy, are squatters, and that don't give us no claim where the company's got a patent to the land."

"If you made a deal with the company, you'd have a patent."

Carrick reached for the bottle and took a long pull. "You're talking crazy now. In the first place nobody like us could deal with the land company. Money's all they want. No matter what you do to improve your place, you get your rump kicked to hellan'gone when they want your land. Second place, this grant was given to a company that never done a thing to earn it. I know 'cause I was supposed to be following the road they built when I came here. Hell, it never was a road. All they done was to pound a few stakes and roll five, six boulders out of the way. Just another land grab."

Morgan could have pointed out that Jim Carrick had settled on the best homesite in the valley, not asking whether it was open to entry or not, but he didn't argue. His own father had done the same and held the same low opinion of the company.

So he built a smoke and shook his head when Carrick offered him the bottle.

"You're sitting between a rock and a hard place, ain't you?"

"That's right," Carrick said gloomily. "We furnish Clancy and his outfit with grain and garden sass and hay. That's free to him for letting us live here. Once a year he butchers and gives every family a quarter of beef. You'd think he was being plumb generous the way he acts. Might as well be living in the old days with a king pushing you 'round. Got so you can't even blow your nose without riding over to Turkey Track and asking old Broad 'bout it." He shook his head. "Now if the company moves in, we won't have nothing."

"Might be you're wrong. Suppose a lot of people move in? It'll bust Turkey Track. You'll have neighbors working for the same thing you are. Won't be long till a railroad is built into the valley and Irish Bend will be a big town."

"Crazy talk," Carrick jeered. "I'll lose this place, won't I?"

"Look, Jim. I own the wagon-road grant. Not somebody back in Boston in a soft-bottomed chair. I want families on this land. I hope to make money and I hope to bust Clancy, but mostly I want folks to develop this valley the way Dad wanted it done."

"I'll be damned." Carrick had started to

lift the bottle again. Now he set it back on the ground, eyes pinned on Morgan. "Yes, sir, I'll be damned."

"This place is on an odd section. That makes it mine, but I don't want to shove you off. I've got a proposition. Interested?"

"You're danged right," Carrick boomed.

"By September 1 the valley will be full of settlers. They've got to be fed. We'll have to haul water for 'em. They'll need horse feed. Maybe there'll be a fight with Turkey Track. I want your help. You give me that help and the day the land sale is finished, I'll hand you a deed to your land."

"Mister, you've made a deal, and I hope there's some fighting."

"What about the others?"

Carrick spat contemptuously. "Like I told you, Royce is no good, and that gal of his is a damned floozy. A Delilah. I like a purty filly same as the next man, but I don't like to see 'em give a wiggle at every man that goes by." Carrick shook his head soberly. "You're bucking a pat hand, Morgan. All of them north rimmers know that the minute they start going agin' Broad Clancy he'll send Rip and Jaggers Flint and a bunch of riders, and every nester in the valley will get cleaned out."

"I'll go see 'em."

"You can count on me and Tom and Buck.

We'll back your play no matter what it buys us."

Morgan leaned back in his chair. He was more tired than he had realized. He felt like a man who has been in a whiplashing gale and will go into it again in a moment, but now sits in a pool of quiet. He looked across the valley toward the Sunset Mountains, rising swiftly above the nearly flat desert, the green pine covering turned blue by the dusty distance.

Here was an open land, a wide land bright with promise. For the moment Morgan let his dreams build. If they held the dark shadow of trouble, it was no more than he could expect. He could cope with trouble when it came; he had been raised with it. He had always been alone; he would be alone now except for the Carricks.

A man could do no more than fight the thing that opposed him, regardless of the form it held. The fun came in the dreaming and the shaping of that dream into the hardness of reality. Someday he might not be alone. A woman gave a fullness to a man's life. He had never known his mother, but from the things his father had told him, she must have been beautiful and good, the kind of woman a man sees in his mind with little hope of finding.

He thought of Jewell Clancy, sweet and fine and practical, but set apart from him because she was named Clancy and he was a Morgan. There was Peg Royce, vibrant and alive, the thought of her enough to send a stirring through him. Carrick had called her a floozy, a Delilah. Buck had said she was a poison. Still, she fastened herself in his mind; he remembered the fragrance of her hair, the pressure of her breasts when she had stood close to him.

Carrick sat in silence, watching Morgan soberly, as if sensing the younger man's thoughts. Now he broke out: "I ain't one to tell another fellow his business, but you'd better get one thing straight now. Don't have no truck with Pete Royce or his gal. They'll sell you out and shoot you in the back. They'll—"

The clatter of horses' hoofs brought Carrick upright. "Tom," he whispered. "He's bringing Buck in. The boy didn't come home last night."

Buck was reeling in the saddle, his face powder gray, blood a black patch on his shirt front.

"Got shot by Rip Clancy last night," Tom Carrick called. "Purty bad. Now you ready to go after the Clancys?"

Jim Carrick swayed drunkenly, a hand gripping a fence post. "Let's get Buck in," he said harshly. "Then I reckon we'll ride." He swung to face Morgan. "Mister, no use putting this off. If you want our help, you'd sure as hell better ride with us."

"That'll wait." Morgan helped Buck down. "Your boy won't."

They carried Buck inside. He was, Morgan

saw, closer to death than he had first thought. He said grimly: "Doc Velie's at the Royce place. If Tom busts the breeze getting there, he can catch him."

"I ain't going after no sawbones," Tom said darkly. "I'm going after Rip Clancy."

"Then you'll have a dead brother. That slug's got to come out of him."

Still Tom hesitated, narrow vindictive face dark with the urge to kill.

"Go on," Jim Carrick said. "Morgan's right."

Tom wheeled out of the cabin. A moment later the thunder of his horse's hoofs came and was slowly muffled by distance and died.

"Kick up your fire." Morgan motioned to the stove. "Get a kettle of water on there and find some clean rags."

Jim Carrick obeyed. Buck lay on the bunk, eyes closed, body slack.

"Can't understand it," Carrick muttered. "Buck went to town yesterday. We've been working purty hard getting the crops in. Tom, he ain't worth a damn here. Hunts and fishes and rides all the time. Ain't no part of a farmer in him, but Buck had a night for howling coming to him. Must have got drunk and jumped Rip."

"Tell him, Buck," Morgan said softly.

Buck stirred, his eyes coming open. "Nothing to tell," he muttered.

"You're forgetting Peg," Morgan pressed.

It was cruel but necessary. The one thing Morgan could not afford now was a showdown fight with Turkey Track. If he rode to town with the Carricks, the only result would be a useless death.

"That Royce gal ain't got nothing to do with his getting shot," Jim Carrick bellowed. "You trying to say she did, Morgan?"

"Go ahead, Buck," Morgan urged, "unless you want me to tell him."

Young Carrick understood. He struggled for a moment with indecision before he said: "I met Peg at the Smith shack. This hombre was there. Rip and his bunch was hunting me. I lined out south, but Rip caught up with me at the lake. We swapped some lead and they got lucky, but I gave 'em the dodge. Fainted once and fell out o' the saddle. Tom found me the other side of Morgan Rock. Couldn't get back on my horse."

Jim Carrick was trembling with rage. He began to curse. "So you're seeing that damned double-crossing floozy . . ."

Morgan came quickly across the room to him. "You trying to kill him, you fool? Tell him it's all right."

Carrick sleeved sweat from his forehead. He swallowed and cleared his throat. "All right, boy. It's all right."

Buck closed his eyes. "I love her, Dad. I'll run away with her if I have to."

Morgan jerked his head at the door. Carrick stepped outside, Morgan following.

"Now get this through your head, Jim. We can ride to town looking for Rip and get ourselves killed, which same won't do no good at all. Buck asked for trouble. If you go off and leave him, he'll die."

"You said yourself a man can stand so much pushing and no more," Carrick flung back. "I've had mine."

"There's no hurry," Morgan urged. "Wait till Buck's on his feet. No sense in getting salivated if it don't do some good."

Carrick wiped a big hand across his face, a driving rage battling his better judgment. "All right," he said at last. "We'll wait, but I won't have him seeing Peg Royce. You hear?"

"Don't tell me," Morgan said softly. "Tell Buck when he's able to listen."

# Chapter 7: The Fight at Blazer's Place

IT WAS NEAR SUNSET WHEN DOC VELIE RODE in with Tom Carrick. He was an old man close to seventy, white whiskered and gaunt with gray eyes that were unusually keen for a man his age. As he shook Morgan's hand, he said: "Been kicking things around for a fellow who's been in the valley less than twenty-four hours. Old Josh Morgan's son, ain't you!"

"That's right."

"You won't live long," Velie said. "Nobody backs Jaggers Flint down, growls at Broad, shoots hell out of Pete Royce and peels Rip's hide off his back and lives to talk about it. You just cut too wide a swath, mister."

Tom Carrick's dour face was momentarily lighted by a rush of admiration. "I figgered you plumb wrong, Morgan. From now on count me in. I want to see things like that."

"You'll see him die," the medico said brusquely. "Come on, Jim. Give me a hand. You two stay outside."

While Doc Velie operated, Morgan told Tom Carrick why he was in the valley and what he hoped to do. Tom swore in delight. "I'd have braced old Broad myself if I had the chance. I ain't cut out for no farmer. Mebbe I'll be a town marshal when Irish Bend spreads out."

"Maybe," Morgan said, and let it go at that. Tom Carrick lacked the cool judgment that a lawman needed, but there was no point in telling him.

Hours later, Doc Velie came out of the cabin, Jim Carrick behind him.

"It'll be close," the medico said. "He's lost a lot of blood and that slug was hard to get. Keep somebody with him all the time, Jim, and don't get him worked up over nothing. Might be a good idea to send for Peg Royce."

"She'll never put a foot in my house," Jim Carrick said darkly.

"All right. Let the boy die." Velie pinned his gaze on Tom who had come to stand in the patch of light washing out through the open door. "If you want Buck to live, quit talking about getting square with Rip Clancy. No sense worrying him with your tough talk."

Without another word Doc Velie strode to his horse, pulled himself into the saddle and rode westward.

"There goes the one man in this valley," Jim Carrick murmured, "who ain't afraid to tell Broad Clancy what he thinks."

The next week was slow and worry plagued. Morgan or Jim Carrick or Tom was always in the cabin or within call. Tom fretted with the

89

inaction, giving less time than either of the others, and the moment he was relieved he'd saddle his horse and thunder out of the yard without a backward glance.

"Always been that way," Jim Carrick said bitterly. "I've been a farmer all my life. Always will be. Like to have my hands on the plow. Like to have my feet in the furrow. Buck's like me." He shook his head, brown eyes turned dull by regret. "But Tom's got wild blood in him. Wants to ride out of the valley and hire his gun. Born to die with lead in his belly, I reckon."

It was not a wasted week for Morgan. He learned the names of the nester families, what each man was like, how far he could be depended upon. He trusted Jim Carrick's judgment; he felt a closeness for, and an understanding of, him as he instinctively felt distrust of Tom. Not of the boy's integrity or loyalty, but his stability, for Tom Carrick was the kind who would throw away his life on a sudden wild impulse, and bitterness over Buck's shooting was a growing cancer in him.

At the end of the week Doc Velie nodded with satisfaction as he made his examination of Buck. "Give him plenty to eat and keep him quiet," he said. "All it takes is time." He winked at Buck. "That's what comes of living right." Outside he laid a hand on Jim's shoulder. "I ain't one to meddle in family business, but Buck ain't gonna

90

get back on his feet like he ought to unless he's got something to live for."

"If you're talking about Peg . . ."

"That's just who I am talking about."

"He's got me to live for," Jim said sourly. "And Tom. He's got the place."

"Damned if you ain't the stubbornest man outside the Clancy family there is in the valley. Jim, try to get this through your thick head. Buck has come mighty close to cashing in. He loves you and Tom, sure. He likes the place, even if it ain't yours, but there's more than that in the living and dying of a man. I don't know what it is, but I've seen it time after time. It's something beyond what any doctor can do. I reckon you'd call it the will to live. Put Peg Royce in this house for a few hours and you'll think it's a miracle. Don't send for her, and you've got a good chance of planting him up there beside the Morgan boys."

It was the longest speech Morgan had heard the medico make. He waited until Velie had gone. Then he said, "Jim, I've got some chores to attend to. I'd like for Tom to notify all the north-rim nesters that there'll be a meeting tonight. Can he see 'em in time?"

"Hell, yes."

"Where'll we have it? Here?"

Carrick shook his head. "It'd be a long ways for some of 'em to come. Let's say Blazer's place.

91

That's central and it'd make him be there." He gave Morgan a straight look. "Be ready for the damnedest fight you ever had. A pair of fists is the only thing that'll make Arch listen."

"Then that's what I'll use." Morgan glanced up at the sun. "Get Tom started. You and me will head out of here 'bout noon."

As Morgan turned toward the corral Carrick called, "Where are you going?"

"After Peg."

Morgan didn't look back. He had learned to know Jim Carrick well, and he measured him as a just man but a stubborn one. He was not sure whether Jim would rather see his son dead or married to Peg Royce. Oddly enough, he never doubted that Peg would come, but when he reined up in front of the Royce cabin, doubts hit him like the rush of cloudburst waters down a dry channel.

Peg was standing there in the doorway, black-haired head tilted against the jamb, the same confident smile on her lips that had been there the first time he had seen her.

"So you came back, Mr. Morgan." She walked quickly across the yard to where he sat his saddle. "Get down. Royce isn't here."

"You heard about Buck?"

She nodded, her face grave. "Doc stops whenever he goes by. He was worried about Buck for awhile."

"He's still worried. When Buck was out of his head, he did a lot of talking about you."

Interest was keen in her dark eyes. "What did he say?"

"He loves you."

"Why, I guess he does."

"He's still pretty bad. We've got to be gone a day or two. Jim wants you to come over and stay with Buck."

She stared at him blankly for a moment before she caught the significance of what he'd said. "I gave up believing in fairies a long time ago, Mr. Morgan. I'd as soon start in now as believe Jim Carrick wanted me in his house."

"It's true."

He had a bad moment then. He wasn't sure Peg believed him and he wasn't sure she'd come. He thought of telling her it was her fault that Buck was shot and knew it wouldn't do. He thought of offering her money and immediately gave the thought up. So he sat looking down at her and saying nothing until she laughed, not the gay laugh he had heard before, but a short bitter one, as if something had hurt her and she was covering it with a show of humor.

"All right. I guess it would be worth riding over there to see the look on Jim Carrick's face when I walk in."

"I'll saddle up for you."

"You could take me up in front."

He said quickly: "This animal won't carry double. I'll saddle up."

She bit her lip, frowning. "I don't usually frighten men."

"I scare easy." Reining around her, he rode to the corral. There was little talk on the way to the Carrick place. Morgan watched her for minutes at a time, but if she was aware of it, she gave no indication. He had never seen, he thought, a prettier girl. Her breasts rose and fell with her breathing; he saw the pulse beat in her white throat. When at last she appeared conscious of his gaze she turned to him, smiling again, and he saw the dimples in her cheeks and the knowledge in her dark eyes.

"Are you going to draw a picture of me?"

"Just store one in my memory. You're Buck's girl."

Quick pleasure stirred her face and then she looked away. "No, not Buck's girl. I'm doing this because you asked me. I thought you knew that."

Again they rode in silence until they reached the poplars in front of the Carrick cabin, and Morgan, stepping down, reached up and helped her from the saddle. Jim Carrick loomed in the doorway, his face set. He said in a dry precise voice: "Come in, Miss Royce. Buck's expecting you."

Morgan put his horse away and waited outside

until Jim called him to dinner. He couldn't guess what had been said and he didn't ask, but there was a look on Buck's lean face that should have told Jim what Morgan already knew. They left shortly after they had eaten, riding northwest across the valley so that they cut between the lake and the barren Alkali Flats.

The sun, its roundness unmarred by clouds, dropped into the western sky, and the wind, cooled by the high Cascades, touched them briefly and passed on, stirring the bunchgrass with its passage. To the south Clancy Mountain was a sharp triangle marking the skyline. The smell of the air was clean and sharp, a good smell rich with sage, a smell Murdo Morgan had almost forgotten, and a hunger to live out his life in the valley struck at him. For a moment he harbored a thought he was afraid to explore. He could have Peg Royce.

"Not many Turkey Track cows in the flat," Carrick said suddenly. "Clancy keeps 'em down through the winter, but his riders have been shoving 'em toward the ranch the last two, three weeks. Reckon he'll be branding afore long."

"How soon will he start 'em for the marsh?"

"Any time. He'll take it easy on the way up. Too much snow to get 'em on the marsh yet. More snow last winter than any year since I've been here."

But Morgan's mind was not on Broad Clancy's

cattle. "You think the nesters'll come tonight?" he asked.

"Sure. They'll come to hear what you've got to say, or to see Blazer stomp you to death. These boys have the notion that if they lick anybody who comes in, they can hold their places." Carrick cocked his head at the sun. "Let's kick up a fire and eat. A man can't fight on an empty stummick."

"How far yet?"

"A mile or so. No sense hurrying. You want all the boys there to see you handle Blazer." Carrick reined up and looked directly at Morgan. "You done wrong, friend, and so did I. We shouldn't have left that girl with Buck."

They built a fire and cooked supper. Then they waited until the sun was behind the Sunset Mountains and dusk flowed across the desert and laid its purple hue upon it. A quietness came with the twilight, a quietness that worked into a man's mind and called up a thousand thoughts and images and dreams. Morgan gave no thought to the fight with Blazer. It was immediate, a little dirty job that had to be done before he could do the big job. He let his thoughts range ahead to the families that would be making their homes in Paradise Valley.

Rising, Morgan tossed his cigarette stub into the fire and kicked the coals out. He said, "Let's ride."

Carrick had been squatting on the other side of the fire, face dark and preoccupied, and Morgan knew he had not shaken Peg Royce out of his mind. Carrick said, "All right." Mounting, they swung around a rock finger that stabbed the valley from the rimrock and saw the red tongue of Blazer's fire.

"Got a good light," Carrick grunted. "Blazer likes to put on a show."

The nester had built the fire in front of his cabin. As Morgan pulled up he saw that the cabin was set hard against the cliff and was built of stone. Blazer, he thought, had an eye more for defense than home comforts.

"Hello," Carrick called.

A dozen men were hunkered in a circle around the fire, Tom Carrick withdrawing from the others and squatting by himself, eyes watchful, jaws working steadily on his quid.

A big man rose and made a slow turn. He said, "Light," his tone heavy and filled with hostility.

Carrick and Morgan dismounted and came into the firelight. Carrick introduced Morgan to each man, holding Blazer back until the last, a gesture of contempt that all understood. When at last Carrick called Blazer by name, Morgan's eyes locked with the big man's, and he made a quick appraisal of him.

Arch Blazer was as tall as Morgan and heavier bodied. His neck was short, his ears small and set tightly against his skull; his yellow eyes were reddened by dust and sun and wind. He stood with shoulders hunched forward, hands fisting and opening, wicked temper showing on his dark face.

"So you're the company man we heard was coming to kick us out of our homes," Blazer growled. "You ain't gonna do no such thing, Morgan. You try it and I'll stomp your guts out."

Morgan ignored it. He made a quick study of the men, thinking how well Jim Carrick had called it. A raggle-taggle outfit if he had ever seen one, scared and ragged and dirty. Hiding from the law and picking up a precarious living from their farms, a living supplemented by deer and antelope and perhaps an occasional Turkey Track steer.

"You know how the valley is held," Morgan said. "Some of you are living on government land. Maybe you've filed on it right and proper. If that's the case I've got work for you and good wages. If you're on company land, I've got the same work to offer and a proposition."

"We don't want no proposition," Blazer growled. "All we want is to be let alone. We ain't leaving our homes so some damned land company can sell 'em when the company stole the land in the first place."

Again Morgan ignored Blazer and kept his

eyes on the others. "I'm the company. The offer I make now goes. It ain't a case of some rooster back East in a plush chair going over my head. By September 1 there'll be thousands of settlers here in the valley. If you men will help me feed 'em, haul water for 'em, and fetch horse feed, I'll hand you a deed to your land the day the sale is finished. No red tape. No monkey business. How about it?"

Blazer wheeled, a great hand motioning toward Morgan. "Don't believe this lying son. How do we know who he is or whether he'll keep his word?"

"I believe him," Jim Carrick said. "I'm done sucking after Broad Clancy. If Morgan puts this land sale over, it'll bust Turkey Track."

Blazer swung on Carrick. "You allus was soft as mush, Jim. I say to run this smooth-talking son out of the valley. I'll plug the first man who sets foot on my place and claims he bought it from the company."

"Then you'll hang for murder," Morgan said quietly.

Blazer threw back his great head and laughed. "Hanging, he says, for murder. You won't be around to see it, Bucko. You won't even be around. I'm gonna bust you up. I'll teach the company to send in a long-tongued rooster, lying about owning it himself."

Morgan jerked off his gun belt and handed it

99

to Carrick. "All right, Blazer. I never look for a fight, but if it comes, I always finish it."

Again Blazer laughed, belly-deep and scornful. "You'll never finish this one, Bucko. I'll have my fun and I'll still be here when your friend Carrick is digging a hole for you."

"If you want some fun, I'll give it to you," Morgan said, and came at the man fast, right fist cracking him hard on the mouth.

It was Arch Blazer's way to bluff as far as he could, to scare a man and make him back up before a crowd and half win the fight before it started. He had never had a man bring the fight to him, and surprise and Morgan's blow half-stunned him for an instant. He retreated a step. Morgan, catching him on the jaw with another short wicked right, knocked him flat on his back.

"Boot him," Jim Carrick called exuberantly.

From the other side of the fire Tom Carrick watched with cool pleasure, for he had long hated Blazer and knew he was not the man to do what Murdo Morgan had just done. The others pressed closer, silent and watchful, swinging the way the fight went.

Blazer hit the ground and bounced up, a strangled curse breaking out of his bruised mouth. He drove at Morgan and struck him a hard blow on the chest. Morgan wheeled and let the weight of Blazer's charge carry him by. He was on the big man then. For an instant Blazer was off balance. Morgan ripped through his guard, punching him with rights and lefts, the huge head weaving from side to side.

Blazer clubbed a fist at Morgan's face and closed with him, swinging a fist into his belly. Morgan was hurt. He threw his weight hard against Blazer, cracking him in the ribs, turned sideways as Blazer rammed a knee at his crotch, and catching the man's leg, dumped him into the hot coals at the edge of the fire. Blazer screamed and rolled clear. He came to his feet again and rammed at Morgan, but he was slower this time; the heart had gone out of his fight.

Sensing the moment, Morgan came in for the kill, fists ringing on Blazer's head, flattening his nose and closing an eye. He saw the man's blood, tasted his own, felt the jar of each blow run up his arm and wondered what held the nester up. Then, for no reason that he could understand, Blazer's knees became rubber and he curled to the ground.

Morgan stepped back, thinking Blazer was out, and instantly knew he'd made a mistake, for Blazer had rolled away from the fire and had drawn gun. Another gun spoke, the bullet kicking up dirt a foot from Blazer's hand.

"You'll fight him fair," Tom Carrick raged. "Damn you for a dirty stinking polecat."

Blazer dropped his gun. He squalled, "I'll get you Carricks for backing—"

Blazer didn't finish. Morgan fell on him, knees hard on the big man's ribs, grabbed a handful of hair and twisted his head so that his chin was a clear target. Morgan swung his right, the sound of the blow a meaty thud of bone on bone. He raised his fist to strike again, heard Jim Carrick cry, "That done it, Murdo." He rose, a boot toe digging into Blazer's ribs, but there was no stirring left in the man.

"Thanks, Tom." Morgan wiped a hand across his bloody, sweaty face, not realizing until then how much he had been hurt. "You boys heard my proposition. Interested?"

"Sure," one said without enthusiasm.

Some nodded, others stood staring at Blazer, as if unable to believe they had seen him beaten.

"All right. If you carry out your end of the bargain, you'll get the patents on your land." Morgan took his gun belt from Carrick and buckled it around him. "Blazer will never get a chance to pull another gun on me when I don't have mine. Tell him he'd better start smoking his iron the next time we meet, 'cause I'll sure as hell be smoking mine."

Morgan lurched to his horse and painfully eased into the saddle. He rode around the finger of rock and presently the Carricks caught him.

"That's a thing I had fun watching," Tom said jubilantly. "Blazer's run over everybody since he's been here."

"What'll he do now?" Morgan asked.

Tom laughed shortly. "Tuck his tail and run. He won't want to swap smoke with you. With him gone, the rest'll be plumb happy to haul your horse feed and water."

Jim Carrick shook his head. "I ain't sure 'bout that, Tom. Not with Pete Royce around."

"I don't think I feel like riding back, Jim," Morgan said.

"There's a spring down here a piece. We'll camp there."

After they had made camp, Morgan lay with his head on his saddle and gave voice to a question that had been nagging his mind. "Some men just like to fight, but I ain't sure Blazer's that kind. The proposition I offered was fair. Why did he jump me thataway?"

"He's just an ornery cuss," Tom said.

"Might be more to it," Jim Carrick said. "He's plumb thick with Royce."

The run of horses came to them, and Morgan murmured, "Some of the boys going home."

"I'll see," Tom said, and mounting, rode off.

"Can't sit still," Jim growled. "Been on the go ever since he could stick in the saddle. Rides most of the time. Knows more about what goes on than anybody else in the valley, unless it's the Clancy girl."

Morgan closed his eyes, utterly weary and weak

with the letdown that follows sharp physical action.

Morgan and Jim Carrick had breakfast at dawn and reached the Carrick place by midmorning.

"Go on in," Carrick said. "I'll take care of the horses."

"No hurry," Morgan said.

Peg was sitting by the bed reading to Buck when Morgan and Carrick went into the cabin. She looked up when she saw them, carefully closed the book, and rose.

"How you feeling, son?" Carrick asked.

"Fine." Buck winked at Peg. "She's the right medicine for a man."

Peg wasn't listening. Her eyes were on Morgan's bruised face, concern in them. She asked, "You had trouble?"

"He licked Blazer," Carrick said.

Peg picked up the scarf she'd worn around her head. "I'll be going."

"Thanks," Jim said carefully. "I'll saddle up for you."

"You'll come back?" Buck asked.

"Sure, I'll be back," Peg said easily, and left the cabin with Jim Carrick.

Morgan idled in the doorway, shoulder blades pressed against the jamb, feeling the soreness that would be days leaving him. He watched Peg mount and wave to him. He raised his hat and nodded, unsmiling. He was thinking again that

104

he could have Peg Royce, and panic was in him with the rush of knowledge that he wanted her.

"Morgan," Buck called.

Morgan walked to the bed and sat down. "Want me to read to you?"

"I told you she was poison," Buck said harshly. "I said she was a fever that got into your blood."

"I remember. Why?"

"You ain't fooling me no more than a little. You're playing smart, going after her and all, but you ain't fooling me."

"What the hell are you talking about?"

"You know all right." Buck's fists clenched above the blanket. "I saw the way she looked at you. She's different than she was before you came. I'm telling you, Morgan. Let her alone or I'll kill you."

# Chapter 8: The Schemes of Little Men

PEG ROYCE DID NOT SLEEP THE NIGHT SHE returned from the Carrick place. Her lean-to room held the day's heat with grim tenacity; the smell of her straw tick was musty and stifling. She lay on her back, motionless, staring at the black ceiling. Tomorrow would be another day, the same routine, the same frustrations, the empty sagebrush miles all around, choking her, imprisoning her, walling her in from the world she had seen in her dreams.

The staccato beat of her clock marked the slow passage of the minutes, while the gray ashes of discontent piled high in her mind.

Daylight wiped the darkness from the corners of the room. Royce was gone. She didn't know where. He was gone when she had come home the day before. It was that way most of the time, one of the few things for which she could be thankful.

She should get up and build the fire. Feed the chickens. Milk the cow. Water the horses. Cook breakfast. She'd get a cursing if Royce came home and found her in bed. Maybe more. Anger smoldered in her. No, nothing more than a cursing. She reached under her pillow and pulled out the small pistol she kept there. She'd never take another beating from Pete Royce.

She should get up, she told herself. She sat on the edge of her bed, took off her nightgown, and lay back. No hurry. What was waiting to be done could keep on waiting. If Royce didn't like it, he could stay home and do the chores himself.

The sun laid a pattern of black and gold across her bed. She propped herself up on an elbow and looked at her slim body. She might as well be a squaw. She had her choice of a cocky kid who wanted her but had never offered her the Clancy name, and Buck Carrick who had planned to kidnap her and take her to Prineville to marry him, a nester whose father didn't even own the land they lived on. Then she thought of Murdo Morgan. But then she had been thinking of Murdo Morgan all night.

Peg had never really known another woman. Her mother was a blurred memory. She was not even sure the woman was her mother. There were a few nester women below the north rim. Dowdy, flat-bosomed women broken to the daily labor of this land, women for whom the flame of life had gone out long ago. Auntie Jones in town. Jewell Clancy, who had left her strictly alone.

There had been men around as long as she could remember. All of them but Ed Cole had run to a type. Like Arch Blazer. Tough and dirty and stinking of whisky and horses and tobacco and stale sweat. Men who had wanted to paw her, men that even Pete Royce did not trust with her. She knew men, knew the urging of their hunger. She had never met a man she could not have had if she had wanted him, even Ed Cole, until Murdo Morgan had ridden into the valley.

She had heard men talk lightly about love, as if it were the same as desire. Probably it was to the men she had known. It would not be with Morgan, but what did he want in a woman that she did not have or could not give him? Now, picturing the tall hard-muscled body, his black hair and highboned face, the powder-gray eyes that seemed to look beyond the limits of ordinary men's vision, she felt an undefined longing that she had never felt before. She asked herself if it was love and suddenly regretted what she had said to him about holding the winning hand on the last deal.

Outside a rooster crowed, a harsh sound that brought her upright in bed. She shook her black hair out of her eyes, slid into her worn slippers and went into the other room. She built a fire, pumped water into the coffeepot and set it on the front of the stove. The pine kindling was exploding with dry crackling pops when she went back into her room.

She sat down in front of her dressing table and began combing her hair. She had made her table, just as she had made everything else in her room except the mirror on the wall that gave back a wavy image of her face. Her dressing table had been a huge goods box. She had built shelves into it, papered the inside with red wallpaper, and covered the top with a flounce of print. She had made the rag rug that covered the floor. It was hers, all of it, a sanctuary where Pete Royce let her alone unless he had work for her to do.

She combed her hair sleekly back from her forehead and tied it with a red ribbon. She dressed slowly and was buttoning the last button when she heard horses. She ran out of the room, a wild hope in her that it would be Morgan. Then disappointment slowed her pulse. One rider was Pete Royce. When they were closer, she saw that the other man was Ed Cole.

Peg was slicing bacon when they came in. She had the table set, the coffee boiling, and Cole stopped in the doorway, sniffing audibly.

"Say, that smells good," Cole said. "Pete, this girl of yours is getting smarter all the time."

"You mean lazier," Royce grunted. "Riding at night. Wanting to sleep all day. I'll have to tan her with a blacksnake so she won't forget who's boss."

Peg wheeled, balancing the razor-sharp hunting knife in her hand. "I've told you, Royce. I'm telling you again. You lay a hand on me and I'll kill you."

Royce dropped into a chair. "See how it is,

Ed? The mountain men had the right idea. Marry a squaw and lodgepole her when she got out of hand." He was under average height, a stocky man with shiny blue eyes set close together astride a flat nose that had been smashed under another's fist years before. He leaned back in his chair and drawing a cigar from his pocket, slid it between dark teeth. "A wilding, this filly. Why don't you marry her and tame her, Ed?"

Cole came across the room to where Peg stood. "That suggestion isn't a bad one. You're lovelier every time I see you. How about going back with me. You'd like San Francisco."

"Royce said something about you marrying me," she said pointedly. "Is this a proposal?"

His smile was a quick amused curve of his lips. "Of course, but it depends on breakfast. I'm hungry enough to eat a curly wolf."

"Bite yourself."

He laughed. "I may be a wolf, but I'm no cannibal."

Cole went back to his seat across from Royce. Peg moved around the table so that she could watch him while she rolled out the biscuits. Cole was thirty-five, the most handsome, perfectly mannered man she had ever known. She had been attracted by him when he had been in the valley before. He had tried to kiss her once and she had slapped him. She had never been sure why, and she didn't know what she'd do if he tried again.

His eyes were blue and as guileless as a child's; his hair was light brown and curly, his teeth white and perfect when he smiled. But Peg Royce understood him well enough to know that he was playing his own sharp game. He had not said anything about taking her to San Francisco the other time he was here. He had his reasons now or he wouldn't have made the offer.

Peg slid the pan of biscuits into the oven, and straightening, scratched her chin, leaving a daub of flour on it. It was her chance. Cole needed Royce and she could force a bargain from him. San Francisco! The city of dreams!

After breakfast Cole came to her and slid an arm around her waist. "About this San Francisco deal. I've got to get back, and I need you here. If I took you now, I wouldn't have time to show you the town."

"Why don't you say you don't want me to go?" Jerking away from him, she moved around the table. "I didn't say I wanted to go, did I?"

He stroked his carefully trimmed mustache, his confident smile fixed on his lips. "You didn't say so, but any woman would."

"You're bragging. Why not take Jewell Clancy?"

"I only take charming women to San Francisco." He laid a pile of gold coins on the table. "Let's not lose sight of the reason I want you to

111

stay here. I'm not a good gambler, Peg. I want it a sure thing, and with Morgan out of the way, the land sale will fizzle out, and my bank will get the road grant."

"She can't do nothing I can't," Pete Royce growled. He picked up the cigar he had been smoking before breakfast and lighted it again. "No use wasting good money on her. She'll just blow it on duds."

"Your daughter has capacities you never will, my friend." Cole brought his eyes back to Peg's face. "Pete tells me you've met Morgan. He's been having a run of luck. If that holds, I'll need you."

"He's got to the end of his luck," Royce said darkly. "He'll never lick Arch Blazer again."

Peg took a sharp breath. So they knew about the fight! Cole was worried or he wouldn't be piling gold on the table in front of her.

"Blazer won't give him another chance. When we see Clancy today, I have a notion old Broad will do the job for us." Cole picked up the gold coins and dropped them again. "Like the sound of that, sweetheart?"

"What do I do to earn it?" she breathed.

"You're my ace in the hole. Suppose Clancy doesn't do the job? Or things don't work right for your dad to stop Morgan's clock? Then you'll step in. You're persuasive, honey. Just give a wiggle of your hips and you'll wangle anything you want out of friend Morgan. Or talk him into a foolish move."

"Like what?"

Cole shrugged. "Like riding to a certain spot where Pete or Blazer could knock him on the head and throw him into the tules for the hogs. How's that, Pete?"

Royce chuckled. "A hell of a good idea."

"How about it, sweetheart?" Cole was watching her closely. "A deal?"

"I couldn't wangle anything out of Morgan."

"You can get anything out of any man if you try," he said impatiently. "Can I depend on you?"

She nodded. "And when this job is finished?"

"San Francisco. I'll have the most charming girl in the city."

A moment later she stood in the doorway watching them ride west toward Irish Bend, the gold clutched in her hand. Cole had kissed her, and this time she had not slapped him.

# Chapter 9: Short Man, Long Shadow

MORGAN STAYED AT CARRICK'S UNTIL BUCK was out of danger. The day he left, young Carrick was sitting on the porch, thin and filled with self-pity, his uncut hair shaggy-long. It would be weeks before he was himself, but there was no more need for Morgan here, and he was beginning to feel the pressure of time.

Jim Carrick watched Morgan saddle his black, more solemn-visaged than usual. He said, "Tom rode off again this morning. He's gonna find the trouble he's looking for if he keeps at it."

Morgan nodded. Tom was all right. It was Buck who worried Morgan. Peg hadn't been back after that one time, and the truth was gnawing at Buck's vitals with terrible tenacity.

"Tom can take care of himself." Morgan led his horse to the trough. "I ain't sure Buck can."

"I ain't neither," Jim said dully. "If it was any other girl . . . Oh, hell, I ain't going after her again. You hear?"

"Your going after her don't change nothing."

"What are you gonna do?"

"I'm aiming to see Broad Clancy first thing.

114

I've got to get this business lined out so there won't be no trouble when the settlers start rolling in."

"Take more'n words to change Clancy's way of seeing things."

Morgan stepped into the saddle. Jim Carrick was right, but if there was fighting to be done, it had better be done now. He said, "Thanks for giving me a hand, Jim."

"Hell, it was you that give me a hand. If you hadn't sat up with Buck, I don't know how I'd made out. Tom wasn't no help."

"You gave me more of a hand than you figgered," Morgan said somberly. "You're the balance wheel in the valley, Jim. I'm counting on you. So long."

Morgan reined his black toward the road. He heard Jim call after him, "Take care of yourself, son." Then sourness was born in Morgan. He raised a hand in farewell to Buck, but young Carrick made no answering gesture. Jealousy stamped a festering bitterness on his face.

Morgan wouldn't stop at the Royce cabin. He'd ride on. Peg was Buck's girl. But when Morgan passed the Royce place, he saw Peg working in the yard. Coming to the road, she waved to him, and despite his promises to himself, he reined over to her.

"It's my friend Murdo," she said. "Come in."

He lifted his hat, eyes on her. She had a firm

curved body and a sort of straightforward daring that he liked. She stirred him now as she always did when he was with her. He said soberly, "Howdy, Peg."

She studied him a moment, a smile striking at the corners of her mouth, but it wasn't, he thought, as confident a smile as she had given him before. Something had happened to her, softening her.

"I've got a pot of coffee on the stove, Murdo. Come in."

He shouldn't go in. She was Buck Carrick's girl. He couldn't forget that. But he did go in, and as he drank the coffee, another thought struck him. Buck said she was his girl, but it wasn't Peg's idea. There was no mistaking what she was trying to tell him.

He finished his coffee and shook his head when she reached for the pot. "I've got to be riding."

"Ed Cole was here the other day," she said suddenly.

"Cole!" He stared at her, surprised that Cole was in the valley. "Does he know I'm here?"

She said, "Yes," her face holding an expression he didn't understand.

"Why didn't he see me?" Morgan asked.

"I guess he didn't want to."

Anger touched him. "I'd want to see a friend if I was this far from home."

"Friend?" She laughed shortly. Then, seeing his face, she shut her lips against what she had meant to say.

"Sure. I knew him in Colorado before I had a notion I'd own the road grant."

He automatically reached for tobacco and paper and twisted a cigarette, puzzling over Cole's reason for being here. The Citizens' Bank had no interest in the grant unless Morgan failed to repay his loan within the specified time, but if Cole had come only out of friendship, he would not have left without seeing him.

Peg moved around the stove to stand near Morgan. There was a new expression in her dark eyes, as if something had disturbed her. She said softly: "I know what you're up against better than you do, Murdo, but there isn't much I can do except to tell you to ride on while you're still alive."

"I won't do that," he said roughly.

"I know." She laid a hand on his arm, making a soft pressure there. She was watching him closely, as if wondering what she should say. "There is something else, Murdo. Don't trust anyone. They're all against you."

The cold cigarette dangled from a corner of his mouth. He fished a match from his pocket, but he didn't bring it to life. He held it there, half-lifted in front of him, his mind trying to pierce the veil behind which she had hidden her thoughts. He said: "A man's got to trust somebody. You can't live alone."

She had told him all she would. A quick smile flowed across her face, warm and compelling; her breasts rose and fell with the increased tempo of her breathing. "You wouldn't have to live alone, Murdo."

He dropped the match and tore the cigarette from his mouth. Gripping her shoulders, he jerked her to him and kissed her, her lips turning up to meet his. They were warm lips, filling him with ancient man hunger as they had filled Buck Carrick and Rip Clancy. He let her go, the thought of the other two filling his mind with gray distaste.

She didn't move back. Her arms were around his neck, her lips parted. He saw that she was pleased with what she had done.

She breathed, "That was what I meant, Murdo."

"You've had your fun," he said roughly. "I guess that was what you wanted."

He wheeled away from her and strode out of the cabin and across the yard to his horse. She ran after him, suddenly fearful. "Murdo, didn't it mean anything to you?"

He didn't answer until he was in the saddle. He said then, "Yeah, it meant something. Made me think of what Buck said."

"What was that?"

"That you're a fever in a man's blood if he

looks at you twice. I made that mistake. One look should have been enough."

"Murdo, this is different. I never promised Buck."

"You're his life," Morgan said soberly. "Why don't you go back and see him?"

"All right," she breathed. "I will because you've asked me."

"Thanks."

Morgan lifted his Stetson and rode on toward Irish Bend, a vague unease in him. She was going to see Buck because Murdo Morgan had asked her to. That left him in her debt and that was not the way he wanted it.

The empty miles dropped away; the lake and the tule-carpeted swamp were lost behind a ridge. A band of horses broke across the road in front of him and thundered on through the sage and rabbit brush toward the pine hills to the south. Morgan was hardly conscious of them. His thoughts were a tumbling stream within him. Peg had wanted to tell him something and then had been afraid to say it, but when he tried to concentrate upon it the memory of her kiss ripped through the pattern of his thoughts.

It was nearly noon when Morgan reached town. He racked his horse in front of the store, gaze sweeping the street. It was the first time he had been in Irish Bend since the day he had come to the valley, but it was entirely different. Then

Turkey Track had been in town. Now Irish Bend was almost empty. A single horse stood in front of the Elite saloon, head down, dozing in the sun. A shortlegged dog padded down the middle of the street, ears proudly erect, as if the town was his by conquest, instead of default.

Turning into the store, Morgan asked for a pencil and sheet of paper. The storeman eyed him a moment speculatively before he slid a stubby pencil and a torn fragment of wrapping paper across the counter.

"That'll do if you ain't fussy," he said, his tone intentionally hostile.

Morgan drew a knife from his pocket and whittled a sharper point to the pencil. "Where is everybody?"

"It's always this way when Turkey Track ain't in town," the storeman said. "The boys are winding up branding today. Reckon they'll be heading out for the high country. Be plumb quiet till they get back."

"Maybe not." Morgan began writing. "You'll have more business this fall than you ever had. Better get stocked up."

The man snorted, started to say something, and then shut his mouth with a click of his ill fitting store teeth. He held his silence until Morgan ordered, "Hang this up where folks can see it."

"The hell I—"

"I said hang it up." Morgan grabbed a handful of the man's shirt and jerked him against the counter. "This has been Broad Clancy's town, but it ain't gonna be much longer. I want that paper hung up."

The storeman turned the paper and read aloud:

"The Cascade & Paradise Land Company announces an auction of its land beginning September 1. Stockmen and settlers desiring to secure title to the company land they have been squatting on are advised to contact Murdo Morgan while he is in the valley. Murdo Morgan, Cascade & Paradise Land Company."

The storeman lifted his eyes to Morgan. "If they're gonna contact you, friend, they'll sure as hell have to hurry, 'cause you won't be around much longer."

"That so?"

"You'll ride out or you'll get run out."

"Let me do the worrying, friend. Where you gonna hang this paper?"

The storekeeper picked it up and jabbed it over a nail behind the tobacco counter. "This is one place they all come."

Morgan nodded. "Is there a lawman in town?"

The storeman's laugh was a contemptuous snort. "You wanting some protection?"

"You'll need the protection if you keep trying to be smart," Morgan said coldly. "It don't fit you, mister."

Humor faded from the storekeeper's eyes as if it had been slapped out of him. Fear touched him, narrowing his eyes and bringing the self-hatred it does to a man when the veneer of his toughness has been stripped from him.

"Abel Purdy," the storeman grunted. "Past the post office."

"Thanks." Morgan swung to the door and pausing, looked back. "If that sign ain't there the next time I come in, I'll hang your hide up in its place and don't you forget it."

The storeman's lips twitched, his sullen curses reaching Morgan only as incoherent growls. Grinning, Morgan turned into the street. Irish Bend had been geared to Broad Clancy's pleasure. The land sale would change that along with everything else in Paradise Valley.

Purdy's place was beyond the post office, a weed-grown vacant lot between. Morgan stepped through the doorway, said "Howdy," and had a quick glance around. There were three straight-backed chairs against the wall, a roll-top desk in the corner covered with a litter of books and papers, and an ancient swivel chair. That was all except for the dust, the splinters of a broken stool in the corner, and Abel Purdy.

"Good morning." Purdy rose and held out his

hand. "I'm Abel Purdy and I believe you are Murdo Morgan. I've heard of you."

Morgan shook the proffered hand. "I ain't surprised. A stranger gets talked about."

"You're like the proverbial new broom, Morgan. Sweeps up a lot of trash until somebody saws off the handle. It isn't much good after that." Purdy motioned to a chair. "Sit down. I never like to talk to a standing man."

Morgan took the chair. He liked Purdy as he had instinctively disliked the smart-aleck storekeeper. Purdy might have been thirty or fifty. It was hard to judge his age. His head seemed to be entirely without hair and was ball-round. Then Morgan saw he was wrong. Purdy had hair, but it was clipped short and was so thin and light-colored that it took a second glance to realize it was there.

"Maybe nobody's gonna saw this broom off," Morgan said.

"Somebody will try." Purdy removed his thick glasses and rubbed his eyes, red-streaked from too much reading, the pupils nearly as colorless as his hair. "Time always catches up with us, Morgan. Broad Clancy thought it never would, but things that happen in the rest of the country will eventually happen here. Half of the valley is owned privately. Ignoring a fact like that doesn't change the fact."

"Well," Morgan said, "I'm glad somebody around here knows that."

123

Purdy laid a marker between the pages of the book he had been reading and closed it. "Intelligence is one thing, Morgan. Emotions that control our conduct are something else."

"You're the law, ain't you?"

"Yes, I'm the law." Purdy's smile was self-mocking. He wiped a sleeve across the shiny star pinned on his shirt. "That, of course, is a figment. All of us here understand the situation. I'm the marshal, the mayor, and the justice of peace. I preside over the town meetings. I arrest a drunk if he is a settler. Then I jail him." He motioned to a door behind him. "We have one cell. I sit as judge if a formal trial is necessary, but a trial is never necessary unless the arrested man is a settler. You understand?"

Morgan nodded. It was plain enough, just as Broad Clancy's rule was plain to see everywhere Morgan looked. "But it's like you said a while ago. Clancy can't change facts by shutting his eyes. The company is selling the wagon-road grant to settlers."

"Perhaps," Purdy said skeptically. "It will take a lot to beat Clancy, and my experience with nesters tells me they won't stand against a show of force."

"This is different, Purdy. We're selling the land now to people in the Middle West. They pay 10 per cent down when they sign their contract and give a note for the balance, payable at the time of the drawing. I'm gambling they'll fight for what they already own."

Interest sharpened in Purdy's pale eyes. "It might work."

"Another thing. This ain't free government land, so we're bound to get a better class of farmers than the usual raggle-taggle outfits that show up every time there is a land rush."

"That might be," Purdy admitted thoughtfully. "Does Clancy know this?"

"I aim to tell him today. He wasn't of a mind to listen the time I saw him in the Silver Spur."

"Let us consider an unfortunate turn in events. Suppose you die?"

"Then I'll be in hell, but the land sale will come off regardless."

"Clancy may have a different idea."

Morgan shrugged. "I aim to keep alive. I didn't come in here to talk about Clancy. What I want to know is this. When the settlers come—that'll be the middle or the last of August—will they get the protection of the law as fully as you can give it?"

Purdy reached for a corncob pipe, his self-mocking smile turning his mouth bitter. "You will have it, as well as I can give it. Notice my qualifications, Morgan. *As well as I can give it.* I'll explain that to you. I have a job. It pays a meager living. I don't know what I'd do or where I'd go if I lost it. Love of security does that for a man, and my security lasts as long as Broad Clancy lasts."

Purdy was making it as plain as he could without admitting completely his own abasement. The hard years had reamed the heart out of this man, leaving only the shell. Rising, Morgan said: "I'll depend on that. Broad may not cut quite as wide a swath in another month or two as he does now."

"Time is a great sea washing in around us," Purdy murmured. "We'll see how well Broad has built his walls. And Morgan, if you're going out to Turkey Track, watch this man Flint. A wounded pride can make even a cowardly man dangerous."

# Chapter 10: Clancy Ears Are Stone

A FAMILIAR SIGHT GREETED MORGAN WHEN he reached Turkey Track, a sight that reminded him strongly of his Montana cowpunching days, for it was a scene that changed only in detail wherever cows were run: the constantly rising dust cloud, the smell of wood smoke from the branding fire, loops snaking out, bawling calves and bawling cows.

It was a sort of organized chaos: half-a-dozen Turkey Track irons in the fire, the rush of smoke as a hot iron burned through hair and into flesh, the smell of it, the smell of blood as knives flashed; Turkey Track run on the left side, under-bit off both ears.

A buckaroo yelled, "Rafter L from Dry Lake."

"Nothing but Turkey Track on this range," Broad Clancy shouted arrogantly. "Put the iron to him."

Stink and sweat, pain and blood, dust and smoke, and over all of it that never-dying bawl of worried cows and scared calves, curses and Broad Clancy's taunting laugh if a rope missed. Throw him. Burn and cut him. Hot iron and steel blade. Drag up another. The cycle repeated until a buckaroo yelled, "This is the one we want."

"Hell, I don't want him. Looks just like the last one to me."

"Sure. It is the last one."

Dusty sweating faces grinning as men stretched and wiped sleeves across cracked-lipped mouths. Somebody kicking out the fires. Cleaning the irons by running them through the dust. Heads sloshed into troughs to come out snorting. Spitting water that was close to mud. A good job well done. Pride here among these knights of gun and horse.

Morgan watching from the fringe of activity, understood and smiled. He'd feel the same as Broad Clancy if he were in Clancy's boots. It was an old scene to Clancy that had been repeated every spring since he had ridden north from California with his herd. Today he had viewed it for the last time if Morgan's plans went unchallenged.

If Morgan had been seen, no one gave the slightest hint. Riders were hazing the cow and calf herd away from the corrals. Broad Clancy, riding a chestnut gelding as only a man can ride who is a cowman born, grinned at young Rip and said something Morgan didn't hear. He motioned to Short John and Jaggers Flint, and as if by previous agreement, the four reined their horses toward Morgan and rode directly to him.

Morgan had remained away from Clancy because he knew that as long as the branding was going on, the little man wouldn't talk. He had waited for a moment that seemed to be the right one, thinking they had been too busy to note his arrival. Now he knew he had been seen from the first and ignored, a common treatment Clancy prescribed for unwanted guests exactly as he had prescribed it for Morgan that first day in the Silver Spur.

Morgan had not come with the intention of fighting. He had avoided it in Irish Bend only by a show of toughness, but young Rip hadn't been there that day, and Rip was the most dangerous man old Broad had. Now, watching them come at him, Morgan had a moment of doubt. Triumph was on Rip's ugly face. Short John, out of place in this tough company, was afraid. Jaggers Flint's muddy brown eyes held the smoldering rage of a man who lacked the cold courage it took to make a play and hated himself for that failing. But it was Short John who surprised Morgan most.

Clancy reined up a dozen steps from Morgan, green eyes grinning from under the bushy gold-brown brows. He had shown a nervous fear that day in the Silver Spur when he had learned Morgan's name. He had not wanted to know Morgan's purpose in coming, assuming it was revenge. Perhaps he had never forgotten the Morgan kid who had left the valley sixteen years before. It might have been that his mind had held the shadowy fear of the boy's return, and he had been shocked by his fear when he discovered that the thing he had been afraid of had become stark reality instead of a black dread held in the recesses of his mind.

Today Broad Clancy was a different man. Morgan saw no fear in him. There was pride, the dignity of a small man who feels his position, the old arrogance that Morgan remembered most of all about him. He seemed entirely sure of himself and his own future, as if Murdo Morgan were nothing more than a bothersome gadfly that could be swept away with a motion of his hand.

"We're busy, Morgan," Clancy said crisply. "What do you want?"

"Trouble," Rip breathed. "Let's give him some."

"Shut up," Broad ordered. "Speak your piece, Morgan. Then git off Turkey Track range. This is wrong ground for you."

Rip was a stick of dynamite, a short fuse sparking. He was the one of the four to watch. Jaggers Flint was the next, but Flint would not start it. Short John wanted none of the trouble, and old Broad, for some reason Morgan did not understand, was filled with a confidence that his position did not warrant.

That was the way Morgan read it, and he hesitated a moment, uncertain what his own play would be. He could beat Rip to the draw and kill him. He was certain of that, and he was equally certain that if it happened, he'd lose the last slim chance of a compromise peace.

"Rip's on the prod," Morgan said at last. "If he pulls his iron and starts smoking, I'll kill him, but that ain't what I want."

"Behave, Rip," Clancy bawled imperiously without looking at the boy. "Talk, Morgan. Damn it, I haven't got all day to sit here."

"You said I was on wrong ground," Morgan said evenly, keeping Rip within range of his vision. "It so happens I'm on my own ground."

Broad Clancy threw back his oversized head and laughed, a belly laugh, as if this were a moment to savor, to be enjoyed to the last full second. "Look, Morgan," he said at last when he could talk. "You surprised me the other day in town. When you said your name was Morgan, I naturally figgered you'd come back to square up for what happened to your brothers. Since then I've learned different. I know why you're here, and you don't scare me worth a damn. I'll tell you why. You haven't got the chance of a snowstorm in hell pulling this off. The Citizens' Bank will close you out and I'll deal with them. That all you got to say?"

Questions prodded Morgan's mind. Clancy knew about the Citizens' Bank, so he must have found out through Cole, but what was back of it? There was no time to consider it now. Morgan said: "Not quite all, Clancy. You've made a lot

131

of money off a range that never belonged to you. I'll give you whatever credit you've got coming for fighting Piutes and the other troubles you had, but those days are gone. You'd be——"

"We're still here," Clancy cut in tauntingly. "One damned company or another has owned the wagon-road grant for years, but my cows keep on eating company grass. I haven't paid a nickel for it and I never will. Now get out."

"Not yet," Morgan said. "I had hoped to make a deal with you. I want everything cleared up before the settlers start coming in. If you want to buy the tract your buildings are on——"

"Save your breath," Clancy jeered. "I'll hold a patent to every acre of company land before I'm done."

"You've had your chance," Morgan said harshly. "You can save part of Turkey Track or you can lose it."

"I'll save all of it and I'll bust you." Suddenly Broad Clancy was deadly serious, the last trace of good humor fading from his wrinkled face. His eyes were emerald slits, the corners of his mouth working under the stress of emotion. "I let you alone after our ruckus in town because I thought you had sense enough to slope out. Now I can see you're short of savvy. You figger you're a tough hand. You got the jump on Rip at Royce's place and you licked Arch Blazer. All right. You've used up your luck. Get out of the valley, or, by hell, I'll hang you with my own hand before I'm done."

"There is such a thing as law," Morgan flung at him. "That law recognizes the right of private property. You ain't as big as . . ."

But no one was listening. Broad and Short John had ridden off after the herd. Rip's prodding laugh cut into Morgan's words. Then he and Jaggers Flint wheeled their horses toward the house.

There was no regret in Murdo Morgan as he sat staring after Broad Clancy and Short John. He'd done all he could. Clancy ears were stone, but why was he so supremely confident? The only answer lay in his certainty of Morgan's failure, and he must have a better reason for that certainty than his belief in himself.

Morgan smoked a cigarette, sitting his saddle there by the corrals. There was no sign of life about the big log and stone house. Rip and Flint had disappeared. Morgan thought of Jewell Clancy. She had offered to help. She was the only one of the Clancys who had foreseen the inevitable pressure of time and what it would do to Turkey Track. He reined his black toward the house. Since he was here he might as well talk to the girl.

Morgan had only seen the Clancy house at a distance. Now that he was here in front of it, he felt his admiration for it. Broad Clancy, coldly self-confident, had picked the spot years before beside a spring where he had wanted to build, the fact that it was company land and not open to entry making no difference to him. Yet he had built well. Morgan, who had seen ranchhouses from the Yellowstone to the Rio Grande, had never seen a better one.

Tying his horse at the pole beyond the row of Lombardy poplars, Morgan's gaze swept the house. It was east of the bunkhouse and cook-shack; the barns and corrals were across the road and a short distance to the south. From its wide porch the Clancys could look across the sage-floored valley to the pine hills and the sharp point of Clancy Mountain. Old Broad had named the peak; it had been his boast that he stood out among men the way Clancy Mountain stood out above the rolling hills.

The house proper was of stone, two stories high, the wings on both sides of lodgepole pine. There was no lawn, but there was a row of hollyhocks along the front of the house. Jewell's work, Morgan thought, an expression of her love for beauty, just as the lawn in front of the Royce cabin was a mark of Peg's character.

Morgan crossed the porch and knocked. The door was open and he could look into the big living room with its tremendous stone fireplace on the opposite wall. Bearskins were on the floor, a scattering of homemade furniture including a sort of divan covered with Navajo blankets, and a collection of firearms on the wall. A man's place, yet clearly marked by a woman's hand.

There was no sound within the cool gloom of the house's interior. Morgan knocked again, louder this time. He heard the pad of feet, and the Chinese cook shuffled into the room.

"Is Miss Jewell here?" Morgan asked.

"Missy out tiding," the Chinaman answered. "Back velly soon. You come in?"

Morgan nodded and stepped inside. The Chinaman pattered on across the room and disappeared. Morgan twisted a smoke, his gaze swinging around the room. A huge picture within a carved walnut frame hung above the fireplace. Broad Clancy's and his wife's wedding picture, Morgan guessed. He had never seen Mrs. Clancy, but now, studying her face, he felt he would not have liked her. Lips too thin, too tightly pressed. He grinned when he looked at Broad's picture. Young, with a long curling mustache, the gold-brown brows not so bushy then, and hair. Plenty of it. But Broad didn't look entirely happy. Sort of disappointed, Morgan told himself. His grin widened. Maybe the picture was taken after they had been married.

Morgan swung around the room. There were other pictures, mostly of the children, but the one in the little office at the end of the long living room shocked him. On the wall above the desk was a picture that was startlingly familiar, so familiar that he thought for a moment it was his own mother. Then he wondered if it could have been her sister.

Taking the tintype of his mother from his pocket, Morgan studied it and then lifted his gaze to the picture on the wall. They were so alike it was fantastic. The only difference was a matter of age. The wall picture was of a younger woman, hardly more than a girl.

A squeak on the floor brought Morgan around, the tintype still in his right hand. In that way he was disarmed, a fact that saved his life. The slightest motion for his gun would have brought death. Rip Clancy stood there, a cocked Colt in his hand, thin face utterly wicked.

"I've been waiting for this ever since you got lucky that day at Peg's place," Rip said with taunting malice. "You ain't as smart as Pap figgers, or you wouldn't have stepped into it."

Jaggers Flint paced forward until he stood beside Rip. He said: "I'll take care of him, Rip. I've done a little waiting, too."

But a vicious cunning had seized Rip. He said: "Not yet, Jaggers. Tie him up. Before we're done with him, he'll make a swap, his land for his life."

"Broad's got some fool notions about how to treat anybody while he's in your house," Flint objected. "He ain't gonna like this. Let's take this huckleberry and dust out of here."

"Pap'll change his mind. . . ." The sound of a horse's hoofs silenced Rip. He wheeled toward the door. "Hell, it's Jewell. Tie Morgan up and dump him into my room. She won't go in there."

# Chapter 11: Death at Turkey Track

JEWELL HAD SEEN MURDO MORGAN RIDE UP to the branding when she was saddling her brown mare. She had hesitated, wondering what had brought him here and knowing the answer at once. This visit had been inevitable from the moment her father had refused to listen to Morgan in town.

For a moment Jewell stood motionless beside the mare, watching Morgan sit his saddle outside the circle of activity. There might be trouble and it was not in her power to prevent it. Mounting, she turned her mare toward the rimrock that formed the north wall of the valley. She rode well, with the easy rhythm of one who had sat in leather before she could walk. A hot dry wind thrust at her and brought her hair down her back and catching it, straightened it out behind her, a filmy gold-bright mass in the sun.

Jewell knew every trail and road in the valley, in the pine hills to the south, in the Sunset Mountains to the west. Nature had endowed her with a throbbing restlessness that daily drove her out of the gloomy house and into the open where the air was thin and clear and pure. She had never understood it, but when the wind gave her its wings and the sunlight painted a distant and beautiful world beyond the far edges of the valley, when the strong sage smell was all around her and the sky was the only roof above her, the restlessness was gone. This was her land and she was its child. But there were the passions of her family to mar perfection. The hidden fears, the huge pride, the false, rooted arrogance: all united to build a shame in her and wrench a protest from her that was wasted.

Usually Jewell rode to the rimrock and worked her way to the top along the snake-wide trail, but not today. She was remembering Ed Cole's visit, her father's grim laugh and growing sureness. Then she remembered Murdo Morgan, tall and square-built, a dark-faced, black-garbed man with a dream greater than any Clancy man had ever dreamed.

The old conflict boiled within her again, loyalty to a family she did not respect against the loyalty to a man she had only briefly met, the man who, as a boy, had been in her thoughts through her growing years.

She reined up in the talus and stepped down. She idled among the boulders, gaze sweeping the gray flat to the pine hills. There, standing as a memorial God had made, was Clancy Mountain. Broad Clancy had committed sacrilege in stealing it.

Jewell had always been honest with herself. She knew how little was the love Broad Clancy had for her, but she did feel a closeness with Short John that she felt with neither Rip nor their father. There was one thing in common between them. They were out of place, tolerated rather than loved. Broad Clancy poured his affection on Rip, seeing in his youngest child much that was in himself. He did not understand Jewell because he did not understand women, and Short John was not tough enough for the position life had given him.

Jewell sat down, hands behind her, eyes on Clancy Mountain. Suddenly she realized, and the knowledge shocked her, that she hated the mountain. Beautiful. Symmetrical. Snow-covered until late spring. A sharp arrow pointing to heaven. She should love it because she loved everything that was beautiful, but she didn't. Abel Purdy had said in a rare burst of frankness that time would consume all of them except old Broad, but the mountain would never allow him to be forgotten. It would be there as long as the earth itself was here.

In that moment Jewell made her decision. If Morgan died today, her hopes died with him. If he lived, he would have whatever help she could give him. Then, with a swift rush of panic, she realized she should have stayed at the branding. She mounted and put her mare at a fast pace back

140

across the valley. The branding was finished. Everyone was gone, but Morgan's big black stood in front of the house.

Jewell ran inside. Morgan must be here. He would never leave his horse. The front room was empty. Disappointment knifed at her. She had hoped to find him waiting. Then she saw Rip in the office. She called, "Where's Morgan?"

"Morgan?" Rip took his boots off the spur-scarred desk and stood up. "How the hell should I know?"

"His horse is in front."

"Which same don't prove a damned thing," Rip said irritably. "Maybe he left his nag and took one of ours. If he did, we'll sure hang him for horse stealing."

That was about as unreasonable a thing as Rip could say. There wasn't an animal on Turkey Track except Flint's sorrel that compared with Morgan's black, but Jewell chose not to press the point. She asked, "You didn't have trouble?"

Rip laughed jeeringly. "Trouble with that big wind? Hell, no. He had something to say about Pap buying land, but Pap told him he'd dicker with the Citizens' Bank when the sign was right like Cole said." He moved to the door. "I'll go look for that hairpin if you want to see him." His face suddenly turned ugly. "Say, you ain't sweet on him, are you?"

"I don't want him murdered. There's enough

141

Morgan blood on Clancy hands now without adding his."

Rip laughed again. "I reckon there'll be some more afore long. Pap should have knowed that pup would grow into a wolf. Now we've got the wolf to kill."

Jewell watched Rip cross to the barn, questions thrusting themselves at her. Turning, her gaze swept the room. Morgan was here, somewhere. Maybe in the barn. Maybe Rip was going to kill him now. She ran upstairs for her gun. Then, in the hall outside the door to Rip's room, she saw Morgan's black Stetson.

Usually Jaggers Flint was with Rip, but she hadn't seen the gunman when she'd come in. Turning into her room, she lifted her short-barreled revolver from the bureau drawer. She saw her hunting knife and on second thought, took it. Jewell Clancy had never killed a man in her life, but she would now if that was what it took to free Morgan. Then a thought paralyzed her with shock. *That man might be her brother Rip!*

Jewell slipped the knife into the waistband of her levis and left her room, a cold purpose ruling her. She moved with cat quiet along the hall, her gun cocked. There was a law in the Clancy house that a bedroom was never entered except upon invitation of its occupant, but Jewell did not hesitate. Gripping the knob of Rip's door, she turned it slowly and shoved the door open with a violent push. She expected to see Jaggers Flint there and she expected to kill him, but the gunman was not in sight. Morgan was on the floor, hands and feet tied, a bandanna gagging him.

For a moment the room turned in front of Jewell. She gripped the foot of Rip's bed, shutting her eyes, faintly aware of an incoherent gurgle from Morgan. She had been keyed to a killing, and now that the killing was not necessary, she stood trembling, tears struggling to break through. Then she gained control of herself, eased down the hammer of her gun, and lifting the knife from her waistband, slashed Morgan's ropes and gag.

He licked dry lips and flexed the muscles of his wrists. "I'm beholden to you—" he began.

"Not here." She gripped his hand and pulled him to the door. "Rip will tear the house down when he finds you're gone."

He was in the hall then and picking up his Stetson. He said, "Careless of Flint to drop it here."

"Flint isn't smart and he was in a hurry, but I'd have found you anyhow. I got back sooner than Rip expected and saw your horse outside." She opened the door of her room and pulled Morgan into it, smiling at his disapproving frown. "A woman's room is no different than any other room, Murdo. Just four walls."

"If Rip found me in here, he'd have some reason to drill me."

"He won't find you," she said, hoping Rip would respect the rule she had not. "This is my one island of refuge."

He stood rubbing his wrists, powder-gray eyes on her. He was, she thought, tough enough to finish the job he had started. This was a world of violent action and brutal force, of blood and dust and sweat. Murdo Morgan fitted into it, but more than that, he had the capacity to adapt himself to any situation. If he survived, there would be another world of quiet and order here in Paradise Valley, a world of turned furrows and filled irrigation ditches and churches and schools. He would fit into that world, too.

"I don't savvy Broad," Morgan said. "He was plumb jumpy when I saw him in town. Wouldn't listen. Just wanted me to get out or get plugged in the back. Today he acted like he had the world by the tail."

"Ed Cole and Pete Royce paid us a visit," she said quietly. "Dad knows why you're here."

"Cole and Royce?" Morgan started to reach for tobacco and paper. Then his hand fell away from his shirt pocket. "What did they want?"

"Cole told Dad that you owned the road grant and had borrowed money from the Citizens' Bank. He said the land was being sold in the Middle West now."

Morgan walked to the window and looked out upon the sage flat, the afternoon sunlight cutting strongly across his face. He asked, "Why did Cole tell Broad that?"

"His bank wants the valley and this is a cheap way to get it. If you fail, the bank will close you out. He said he knew how to make you fail, but if his plans didn't work, he wanted Dad to help."

"What's in it for Broad?"

"Cole promised to see that Dad got title to the land he needed in return for helping break you."

She saw the misery that was in him, saw it tighten his mouth and narrow his eyes, saw the beat of his temple pulse. Ed Cole had bragged that Morgan was a trusting fool who wouldn't suspect him because they were friends, and she sensed the hurt that was in Morgan. He was the kind of man who would give everything to a friend and, for that same reason, expected the best from those he called friends.

Jewell stood at the door, watching him and saying nothing, knowing that he had to work this out with himself. He had, she thought, expected trouble with some of the nesters like Pete Royce; he would have expected trouble with Turkey Track, but he would not have anticipated this fight with the man who had negotiated his loan and called it an act of friendship.

Morgan turned suddenly to face her. "I came

to the house to see you, but I guess there ain't anything you can do. I might as well drift."

"You can't go now," she cried. "Flint and Rip are outside and you haven't got your gun. Wait till dark. I'll find your horse and you can go out through this window."

He gave her a queer grin that might have meant anything. "I've been in some tight spots that looked pretty tough, but I never saw one so tough I had to sneak out through a woman's window."

Crazy, but it was the way Murdo Morgan would feel. She moved quickly to stand against the door, searching for something that would hold him.

"How did Rip happen to get the drop on you?" she asked.

He was halfway across the room when she asked that. He stopped as if suddenly remembering something. "I was looking at a picture on the wall of Broad's office. She looked a lot like my mother."

"She was your mother," Jewell said quietly.

He rubbed the back of his neck, staring blankly at her while his mind grappled with what she had said. He asked, "How did Broad get it?"

"I told you there were two sides to this thing. Dad loved your mother in California, but your father won her. Dad never forgave him. He married right after that, but he didn't love my mother."

"Then that's the reason Broad and Dad hated each other."

"Most of it. The rest was Dad thinking your father came here to flaunt his victory. Dad left California to get away from the Morgans and try to forget your mother."

Outside a man called, "Where's Morgan?"

Morgan wheeled to the window, Jewell a step behind him. Tom Carrick stood in the yard with the sun to his back, slim and arrow straight, hand splayed over gun butt. Rip stepped out of the house and paced slowly toward the other. Jewell gripped Morgan's arm. She sensed what was coming and she knew Morgan did.

"The damn fool," Morgan breathed. "Had to keep looking for his trouble till he found it."

Rip called tauntingly, "What do you want Morgan for, you yellow-bellied clodbuster?"

"Don't call me yellow," Carrick bellowed. "There's Morgan's horse. Abel Purdy said he was coming out here."

Morgan tried to raise the window, but it was solid. Jewell handed him her gun. Taking it, he wheeled toward the door, but it was too late. Rip had pulled his Colt, confident of his superiority over this brash nester. Jewell opened her mouth to scream, but no sound came. Something gripped her throat. Rip had made the wrong guess. Tom Carrick's gun spoke before Rip's was clear of leather and Rip Clancy, his Colt unfired, folded into the hoof-churned dust. Morgan whirled back to the window when he heard the shot. That was when Jaggers Flint, shooting from the barn across the road, cut Tom Carrick down with a shot in the back.

Morgan kicked out the window, Jewell's small gun in his big fist. "Stand where you are, Flint. You'll hang for murder."

Jewell glimpsed the gunman's upturned face, squeezed tight with the panic that Morgan's voice had stirred in him. He tilted his gun and fired. Morgan pushed Jewell away. She fell across the bed and coming back to her feet, saw the splintered slice that Flint's bullet had made along the edge of the window casing; she heard her gun in Morgan's hand and smelled the burned powder.

Morgan wheeled out of the room, calling, "Stay here. I'll get Flint."

She came back to the window just as Flint swung aboard his sorrel and broke out of the ranchyard in a wild run. She heard Morgan pound down the stairs and across the living room, heard her gun talk again and saw that he had missed. Morgan stooped beside Rip, felt of his wrist and seeing his gun in the dead man's waistband, lifted it, and slid it into his holster. He knelt at Carrick's side and turning, waved for her to stay inside. She knew then that both were dead.

"Flint will head for the lava flow," Jewell cried.

She didn't wait for Morgan to ask where it was. She walked out of the room slowly, her legs stiff and without feeling, an emptiness in her. When she reached the front porch, Morgan was in his saddle and cracking steel to his horse.

Jewell stood watching him, worry a sharp pain in her chest. She knew that only one would come back. Then she moved off the porch and through the dust to Rip. Oddly enough, her thoughts fastened upon her father. She wondered what he would do now that Rip was dead.

# Chapter 12: Chase

WITHIN THE FIRST FEW MINUTES MORGAN knew that Flint's sorrel was faster than his black. The black, he judged, had better staying powers, but it was evening, with darkness not many hours away. Then Flint would have the world in which to hide.

Morgan had taken time to throw a shot after Flint. More time to see if Rip and Tom Carrick were beyond help. More seconds before he could hit his saddle. It had added up to precious minutes that had given Flint a good lead, a lead that was steadily increasing. Morgan pulled his black to a slower pace when he saw that he could not close the gap and settled down to a dogged pursuit. Flint would run his horse to death the way he was going. There would be time then for the reckoning.

Flint was quartering across the valley to the northeast. The direction surprised Morgan. The Sunset Mountains lay to the west, a natural hiding place for a man on the dodge. Jewell had thought he would head for the mountains, for she had yelled something about the lava flow. Then Morgan guessed what was in Flint's mind. He was trying for Arch Blazer's cabin

150

below the north wall. Blazer was his natural ally. Pete Royce might be there, too, and Flint was gambling on their help.

An hour passed. Then two, and the sun was dipping behind the crest of the mountains. The gap had widened until Flint was little more than a dot ahead in the sage and grass sea. Blazer's cabin was to Morgan's left, but Flint was keeping a straight course across Alkali Flats, and Morgan began wondering if he had guessed wrong on the man's reason for taking this direction.

Then Morgan reached the Flats, a lifeless desert set here along the north edge of the valley, the surface throwing back a hideous glare with the slanting sunlight upon it. Morgan pulled his horse to a stop and sat slack in the saddle, gaze sweeping around the base of the rimrock, a sourness washing through him.

The silence was deep, striking Morgan with a sudden sense of awesome remoteness. He had never been on the Flats before, although he remembered seeing them when he was a boy. It had been, he thought, the bottom of some ancient evaporated lake, but now it was dry except for a few stinking pools remaining from the spring rains, the crust cracked and broken into irregularly shaped blocks.

Morgan turned his horse toward the rimrock, Flint's disappearance puzzling him. A coyote appeared ahead, a furtive gray shadow, looked at Morgan once, and slipped out of sight among the rocks at the edge of the alkali. Morgan skirted a stagnant pool as an avocet flew upward, its melancholy cry lingering behind it.

Reaching the north side of the flat, he rode up a sharp pitch, and understood what had happened. He had been in the bottom of a saucerlike depression, a ridge of sand to the north blotting out his view. Flint had swung behind that ridge and had cut directly toward Blazer's cabin. Morgan crossed his tracks and reined left, wondering what had made Flint change direction.

The light was thin now, the sun lost from sight with only a golden haze above the mountains lingering evidence of its going. Morgan rode around the finger of rock east of Blazer's place, and pulled up, the cabin bulking before him. He sat motionless for a moment, his eyes trying to pick up some hint of Flint's presence, and failing.

If Blazer was inside with Flint, it would be suicide to come closer. If, on the other hand, Flint had gone on, every moment that Morgan waited meant that the killer was increasing his chance of escape.

Morgan smoked a cigarette, considering this. Flint would be hungry. His horse would be about done. The logical thing was for him to hole up here and hope that his pursuer would walk into his gun.

Morgan swung away from the rimrock, keeping

out of gun range. It was completely dark by the time he had reached the west side of the cabin and still there was no indication that Flint had sought refuge there. Waiting was not a thing Morgan did well, but he couldn't go on until he was certain what Flint had done.

Dismounting, Morgan bellied through the boulders toward the cabin, stopping often to listen, but there was no sound except a coyote howl from some distant point on the rim and his own breathing. A prickle slid along his spine. If Flint was inside, he would hear him and be waiting with a cocked gun.

That would be Jaggers Flint's way, the way he had killed Tom Carrick.

Rage grew in Murdo Morgan then. Tom Carrick had been a queer one, wanting the glory that gun skill gave a man. There might be some question of the motive that had taken him to Turkey Track, whether to give Morgan a hand or to secure the fame that smoking down a Clancy would gain for him. Either way he had proved his courage and skill in beating Rip to the draw. He deserved a better death than a shot in the back.

Morgan rose and plunged toward the cabin, boots digging into the sand. Reaching the front wall, he paused beside the open door to listen. There was no break in the quiet. He tossed a rock inside. Flint, tense and expectant, would fire at the racket if Morgan read him right. Still there was no sound. He slid through the door, and stood listening, gun in hand. He waited another slow minute and risked a match. The room was empty.

Wheeling out of the cabin, Morgan ran to his black, mounted, and pointed him west. He swore bitterly when he considered the time he had lost, but thinking back over it, he knew he had not made a mistake.

Flint was an hour, perhaps two, ahead of him, but sooner or later he would have to stop. The one question for which Morgan's thinking could find no adequate answer was Flint's reason for crossing Alkali Flats and then swinging sharply to his left. Perhaps he was so panicky he was out of his head, but Morgan, considering his native cunning, decided against it. The man had his plan and there was no guessing it.

The hours slid by, starlight a faint glow on the black earth. A cold wind sliced across the valley from the Sunset Mountains, and Morgan, shivering, hunched his shoulders. Presently a light appeared ahead of him. A settler's cabin, he thought, remembering that Jim Carrick had said there were several in this corner of the valley.

When Morgan was close, he called, "Hello, the cabin."

The door swung open, lamplight washing out into the night. An old man stood in the door-way, gnarled and humpbacked, as misshapen as a wind-turned juniper. He shouted, "Who is it?"

"Morgan."

He heard a sigh break out of the old man, heard him say reverently and unexpectedly, "Thank God. Come in, Mr. Morgan. Come in."

It could be a trap. Morgan swung in beside the panel of light and dismounted, gun in hand. The settler, sensing his motion, cried: "You're safe here, Mr. Morgan. Flint's gone. Made me feed him. Rode his horse to death and stole mine. I'm not one to give that kind of a varmint any help I don't have to."

There was a ring of sincerity in the old man's voice. Morgan stepped into the cabin, the smell of coffee strong and inviting. The oldster bustled around the stove. "I knowed you'd be along, Mr. Morgan. Flint, he let it slip you was on his tail." He poured coffee into a tin cup. "I'll let this bacon fry while I go tend to your horse."

Morgan walked around the cabin, stretching tired muscles, drank the coffee, and helped himself to another cup.

Within a few minutes the settler was back. He said: "If you don't catch Flint, I reckon he'll die o' heart failure. Looked to me like you'd scared him mighty nigh to death. Never seen a man boogered like he was. Fingers shaking so he couldn't roll a cigarette. Had his gun on me and jumping like he had chills'n fever. Made me saddle my horse. Wasn't no fine animal, but he

was the only saddler I had. You bring him back if
you find him, will you?"

"Sure, Mr. . . ."

"Mossbrain. Just Mossbrain." The old man
cackled. "I'm like a lot of the sodbusters. Got a
back trail I don't want nobody looking at. Been
scared you'd fetch in a U.S. marshal, but Jim, he
says you won't."

"I figgered you wouldn't want one nosing
around," Morgan said.

"That's right. It'll pay you, friend." Mossbrain
forked bacon into a plate and broke four eggs
into the pan. "We uns don't like Arch Blazer and
we don't like Pete Royce. Don't like Ed Cole,
neither. Too damned slick. So I says to myself,
if I can give this man Morgan a hand, I sure will.
Now you eat, catch some shut-eye, and tomorrow
you'll cut sign, I betcha."

Morgan ate hungrily, thinking that the lines
were more clearly drawn in the nester colony
than he had realized.

"Flint couldn't help bragging some," Mossbrain
rattled on. "Said he drilled Tom Carrick."

"In the back."

Mossbrain swore vehemently. "The heller
didn't tell me that. Old Jim's gonna take that
plumb hard. Mighty fine gent, Jim is. Only feller
in the valley everybody trusts 'cept Doc Velie.
Say, Flint foxed you some. Bragged 'bout cutting
across the Flats so you'd think he'd gone on into

156

the Hagerman Hills. Then he swung back, aiming to git Blazer to help him, but Blazer was gone. Reckon that was what boogered him. Can't figger out why he didn't light out after Broad Clancy. You never would have nabbed him then."

"Maybe he figgered Broad wouldn't cotton to him shooting a man in the back," Morgan said.

Mossbrain looked at him skeptically. "Well, you'll see what happens when Broad finds out Rip's dead."

Morgan rose and twisted a smoke. "I'm afraid of that," he admitted. "Hope he won't take it out on Jim."

"You stay here till sunup . . ."

Morgan shook his head. "I've got to keep going. I owe that to Jim. Thanks for . . ."

"Thanks nuthin'," Mossbrain growled. "I just hope you catch that varmint. You know where he'll be?"

"No."

"I can make a mighty good guess. Hawk's Nest. That rock point you seen when you rode into the valley. South of the road a piece. Remember?" When Morgan nodded, the old man went on, "Wal', just this side of the Nest you'll find a lava flow. Can't track a man across it. There's a spring back in there a piece. If he gets into that lava, you'll have a hell of a time smoking him out. Caves and such."

"Thanks," Morgan said, and left the cabin.

Mossbrain called, "Head south when you get to the rim. By sunup you'll be nigh the Nest."

"Thanks," Morgan said again, and mounting, turned his black up the twisting trail.

Mossbrain had been right. Sunup found Morgan in the first fringe of timber. Daylight showed gray and then sharply red, shadows reluctantly fading from the pine-covered hills and draws. Hawk's Nest, a rugged point of rock rising above the more gently sloping foothills, was an unmistakable landmark ahead of him.

Sunlight crawled along the hillsides and into the draws, and slowly warmed, baking the chill from the night ride out of Morgan's muscles. The lava flow loomed ahead, a black twisting ridge that had been spewed out of some near-by crater in prehistoric times as a molten mass, and cooling, had formed this nearly lifeless desert in which only a few stunted trees found precarious footing.

Flint was here! The closeness of his presence sent a warning impulse along Morgan's nerves. He drew Colt, eyes scanning the lava. A million places there where the gunman could hide while he laid his sights on the man he wanted to kill.

Something had warned Morgan and his mind sought the source of that warning. It might have been the chattering of a squirrel or a jay, a deer bounding through the timber. Then he caught it, the faint reflection of the sun on a rifle barrel poked through a hole in the lava ahead of him.

He went out of his saddle in a long leap, trying for a pine to his left. He heard the rifle crack, the snap of the bullet above him, and he lunged for the tree. He stumbled and fell, hard, the violence of the fall jarring his breath out of him. A second bullet beat up a geyser of dirt and pine needles two feet from his head.

Morgan lay there, struggling to get his wind back, knowing that he made too big a target for Flint to keep on missing. He brought himself to hands and knees, sucking for breath, and coming on to his feet, plunged toward the pine. Then Flint, taking his time with this shot, hit him in the left shoulder, and knocked him flat.

Flint should have killed him then. It came again, the dry sharp crack of the Winchester, the snap of the bullet. It was wide, for the killer, certain of his man this time, had fired too fast. Then Morgan reached the tree and dropped into a depression behind it, pulling air into aching lungs that had not been filled since he had fallen.

Morgan lay on his belly, sick with the realization that death had missed him by inches. It had been the simplest kind of ambush; he had known what Flint would do, and still he had gone into it, for he had had no choice.

*He was still alive!* That was the important thing, for a dead man could not do what had to be done. He thought of Tom Carrick, and hatred for Flint washed through his veins, bitter and implacable. The gunman would not have another chance. Then Morgan felt the blood from his shoulder wound and knew the sickness that had worked into him came from a more tangible cause than relief.

Boots scraped on the lava. Rocks loosened by a man's feet clattered down the steep slope. *Flint was coming after him!* On first thought it seemed to Morgan that the gunman's actions were utterly brainless. He would have done well to ride on. He could have told from the way Morgan fell that there would be no pursuit.

Morgan, gun still palmed, eased back the hammer, ears keened for sound of the man's movements. He was surprised at Flint showing himself. Then he thought he understood. Flint had to make certain. The rawhiding Morgan had given him in Irish Bend had been a vicious goad in his memory since the day it had happened.

Now Flint's steps were lost to Morgan. There was only silence, wilderness silence, and Morgan's nerves tightened with the waiting until he thought he would cry out, or plunge out of the hole, his gun speaking. He forced himself to keep silent while the seconds ticked away. He heard his horse nicker downslope from him, and there was silence again until a redheaded woodpecker started his racketing in the pine to Morgan's right.

The woodpecker flew away, and again time

ribboned out until the waiting was unbearable. Flint was somewhere between the lava flow and the pine tree, too cautious to come into view and still reluctant to leave until he had dug a toe into Morgan's ribs and made sure of his death. Morgan was pinned. The first stirring on his part would bring more of Flint's lead.

Morgan knew he could not wait any longer like this. Movement, any kind of movement was better than lying here in a hole while strength bled out of him. Hatred had died. Instead he felt a driving sense of urgency. Here was a job that had to be done. Jim Carrick was his friend and Tom was Carrick's son. It seemed to Morgan, then, that his own death was not so important. Squaring up for Tom Carrick's murder was.

Morgan tensed himself, aiming to plunge over the rim of the depression and start shooting. The next instant he relaxed, listening. Flint was moving downslope toward Morgan's horse. He thought he was imagining it at first, that his wound and the pressure of danger had made him lightheaded. But it was not his imagination. There was no mistaking the sound of Flint's boots in the lava. Flint had broken and was moving away rather than gamble on rushing Morgan. Or, and Morgan decided that this was the answer, Flint was working toward the horse. Mossbrain's animal had injured himself on the lava or had proved too poor for Flint's flight.

There could be no more waiting. Morgan struggled upright. Swaying dizzily, he leaned a shoulder against the trunk of the pine. Flint must have decided that Morgan was dead or unconscious, for he was hurrying toward the black and paying no attention to the man behind him.

"I never shoot a man in the back, Flint," Morgan called. "Turn around."

The gunman wheeled, surprise shocking him into immobility, lips parted as he stared at Morgan. In that moment all the evil of the man's past had caught up with him. It showed in his eyes, the fear, the knowledge of death that was here for him, the wild clawing for hope and the certainty of his own failure.

"You went down like a dead man, Morgan," Flint squalled. "You're dead."

"Takes more'n a ghost to shoot a man," Morgan said. "I aim to shoot you."

Flint dug for his gun, lunging toward Morgan in a wild senseless leap, panic gripping him. He got in one shot, a hurried desperate one, far wide of the mark. Morgan's first bullet knocked him off his feet. He fought back up to his knees and tilted his gun, struggling for strength to pull the trigger.

Morgan fired again, and missed. Then Flint shot, the bullet barking the tree above Morgan's head. Morgan eared the hammer back and caught

Flint in his sights. The gunman was trying for another shot, but the gun seemed too heavy for him. Morgan fired, the sound of it beating against his ears. Flint's body gave under the impact of the bullet. He fell flat against the earth, fingers slack, the power of self-movement forever gone from him.

The hillside began to buckle before Morgan, now that the job was done. He wanted to look at Flint, to carry with him if he died the sure knowledge that Flint would never shoot another man in the back. He struggled with his sagging body, desire beating through him, but strength was gone.

He saw Flint's body from a distance. He felt strangely detached, as if he were floating, as if space were unmarked by boundaries. His gun dribbled out of his hand and he clutched the pine trunk for support. Then his fingers loosened their grip, and he fell, his blood forming a slowly spreading stain on his shirt. His shoulders ached with hammering throbs, and the smell of pine needles was a pitchy fragrance in his nostrils.

# Chapter 13: Hideout

MORGAN LAY THERE A MOMENT, AN INNER warning beating in his mind. When he tried to get up, he found that his left arm was useless. He realized vaguely that he had to stop the blood and worked his bandanna out of his pocket. Rolling it into a ball, he slid it inside his shirt. He lay there, gritting his teeth against the pain that was rocketing through his body.

The warning still tugged at his foggy consciousness. Then he knew. A horse was coming upslope. He picked up his gun and fumbled two new loads into the cylinder. The horse was closer. A little below where Flint lay. Morgan tried to think who it would be. Old Broad. Short John. Or some Turkey Track hand. They had heard the shooting. They were after him.

The horse stopped. The man was bellying up on him, Morgan thought. He was still in the depression behind the pine tree. Whoever was out there couldn't see him until he was close. Morgan would get him then. He struggled with the hammer of his gun, finally forcing it back. He held the Colt loosely, pointing the barrel up, trying to pick out the sound of movement and all the time knowing it was no use. He couldn't hit anybody if he had a shotgun. He remembered Abel Purdy asking, "Suppose you die?" and his answer, "I'll be in hell, but the land sale will come off regardless." He wondered now if it would. He wished he had written to Grant Gardner.

"Murdo."

It was Jewell Clancy's voice. He did not try to understand why she was here. He accepted the fact that she was. He thought he shouted, "Here," but the word came from his throat in a hoarse whisper.

He heard her quick steps in the pine needles. She was looking down at him, face grave with concern. When she saw the bump his bandanna made under his blood-soaked shirt, she cried: "You're hurt. Stay there. I'll get your horse."

"Can't ride," he muttered thickly.

"You've got to. Dad's coming. He's got a dozen men. He thinks you killed Rip."

She was gone then. Morgan eased down the hammer of his gun and slid it back into leather. It was no use. A wounded man on a tired horse didn't have a chance outriding Broad Clancy and his crew. Clancy probably wouldn't believe Jewell if she told him how Rip was killed. Clancy wanted Murdo Morgan out of the way, and this was a means to that end.

Morgan closed his eyes, tired and sick and without strength. He heard his horse, heard Jewell say, "Get up."

He opened his eyes. The black was beside him, Jewell reaching down to grip his right hand. He mumbled: "Go on. Broad'll kill you for helping me."

"Get up."

"I'll fight 'em here."

"You fool," Jewell cried. "Get up. There's a cave in the lava where we can hide. Get on your feet."

He tried, driven by the compulsion of her words. Gripping the stirrup, he struggled upright. He swayed there, his shoulder a great throbbing ache. He felt the warmth of flowing blood again, and it seemed to him that no man could lose as much blood as he had and live.

"No use," Morgan muttered. "I'll . . . fight . . . 'em . . . here."

"Try." Jewell shook him. "Get into the saddle."

He made his try. Foot in the stirrup. Right hand gripping the horn. There he stayed, for there was no power in his legs.

"Get up," Jewell cried. "You've got to work at it, Murdo."

She was lifting him. Shoving him. Begging him. Somehow he got into the saddle. He sat limp, bent over the horn, more tired than he had ever been in his life, beads of sweat on his face shining against his dark skin.

"This way," Jewell called and ran to her mare.

Morgan put his horse up the short slope and

past the pine, right hand gripping the horn, left entirely useless. He saw Jewell step into leather and wave toward the bleak lava flow. He couldn't get his horse on top of that ridge. He couldn't think past this moment. Why was he running? Who was after him? Why couldn't he stay here and sleep?

He cursed his weakness, cursed his foggy memory, and somehow kept his seat as his horse lurched up the bank of rough lava. Then they were on top of the flow and Jewell's words beat at him from a great distance, "It isn't far. Keep coming. It isn't far."

It was a million miles. They were still on the lava. It was all around, a black desert, rough and broken with strange twisted shapes that looked like a literal hell.

A great hole opened before them. Jewell was riding down into it. He tried to call out, tried to tell her to come back, but the sound that came from his throat was only sound and not words. His black was going down into the hole. Crazy. Hiding in a hole. They'd never get out. He had got Jewell into this. Old Broad would . . . Broad? Who the hell was Broad? He'd ask Jewell.

They had reached the bottom. They were out of the sunlight. It was cool and half dark. Jewell was gripping his right arm. "This is where we stay, Murdo. Dad won't find us. Get down."

He fell out of the saddle, sideways, all control

of himself gone. Jewell tried to hold him, but his limp weight was too much. He hit hard on his side, pain rocketing through him and exploding before his eyes in a million red and orange spots. He lay there, eyes closed, slack-muscled.

For a moment Jewell stood looking down at him, his gray face, dusty and stubble covered, blood from his wound streaking his cheek where he had rubbed his face. She stripped the saddle from the black, slipped it under his head and covered him with the blanket. By that time she had made her decision. Mounting, she rode out of the cave.

It was dark when Morgan came to. He lay motionless for a time, aware of the throbbing pain, of his thirst. He tried to remember what had happened. It came to him slowly in nightmarish flashes, and then he wasn't sure whether he was remembering reality or scenes from a strange and horrible dream.

Time made a slow unmeasured passage. He called, "Jewell." There was no answer. He struck a match, the blaze raveling up into a tiny hole in the blackness. He was lying on a rock floor. The wall, curving upward to his right, was of rock. He knew, then, he was in the cave where Jewell had taken him. She was gone. He puzzled over that. His first thought was that she had gone to tell her father and instantly knew that was wrong. Jewell was a Clancy only in name.

There was one other answer. She had gone for help. Hopelessness washed over him. There was no help for Murdo Morgan on this range. Some of the settlers were for him. Jim Carrick. Mossbrain. A few of the others. He thought fleetingly of Peg. None of them could fight Broad Clancy. Abel Purdy? He swore bitterly. No help from him.

Morgan rolled a smoke, fumbling in the dark, awkward with his one good hand, every movement sending waves of pain through his aching body. He lighted a match and held it to his cigarette. He laid the match down and pulled his watch from his pocket, but before he could catch the time, the match winked out. He lighted another. Two. Morning, he thought, dark as it was.

He heard his horse stomp behind him. No use staying here. He would starve to death. Better get some miles between him and Turkey Track. He could find a doctor at Prineville. When he could fight, he'd be back. He turned on his right side and putting his hand on the ground, brought himself to his knees. Then strength went out of his arm and legs and he dropped back.

That was when he first heard the sound. Rock grating on rock. The rumble of a small slide. The dry smell of dust filtered back to him. He heard a man's grumbled oath and a woman's voice. Jewell! Something stirred inside him. Jewell had come back.

A small ray of sunlight streamed into the cave. More rumbling of rocks. The hole grew bigger. It was daytime. He knew then what had happened. The mouth of the cave had been sealed with rocks.

Minutes later the hole was wide enough for Jewell and Doc Velie to crawl through. The medico, kneeling beside Morgan, taunted: "You're not so tough, friend. I told you you were cutting too wide a swath."

"You said I wouldn't live long," Morgan muttered.

"What makes you think you will?"

"Doc," Jewell cried.

Velie chuckled. "Don't you worry none. This rooster's too tough to die today, but another slug might do the job. H'm. Bullet went through him like a hot knife through butter. Hell, girl, what'd you have me ride out here just to look at this bullet hole for? I've seen better ones."

Afterward, when the wound had been cleaned and dressed, Jewell built a fire and cooked a meal. Doc Velie lighted his pipe and sat against the wall of the cave. He said, "I got a letter for you, son."

"Let's see it."

"I'll read it to you." Velie drew an envelope from his pocket and ripped off the end. "It's from a gent named Grant Gardner in San Francisco. Know him?"

"I know him. Go on. Read it."

Velie held the sheet close to the flames so that the meager light fell across it.

"DEAR MORGAN:

"I am glad to report that the sale of your land grant in the Middle West is progressing faster than we could reasonably expect. It looks now as if every contract will be taken by the first of August. I expect to be in Irish Bend around the middle of the month, and we will make definite plans for the drawing at that time. I have a crew of men who are experts in such matters and have already given them orders to be in Irish Bend the last of August with their equipment, so there will be nothing for you to do except to see that the peace is kept."

Velie laid the letter down. "Son, in case you didn't know it, that little business of keeping the peace will be quite a chore."

"Go on," Morgan grunted.

"I am happy to say that I am much more optimistic about the success of your venture than I was at the time we talked in my office. There are two reasons for my optimism. One is the success of the sale of your contracts which can be accounted for by the dry years and bad crops in much of the Middle West. The second is your own record. I have checked it carefully. If this project fails, I hope you will consider taking a job in my organization.

Cordially,<br>GRANT GARDNER."

Velie slid the letter back into the envelope. "Who is this Gardner?"

"A millionaire," Morgan said. "His business is developing farm colonies."

Velie reached for his pipe. "How do you expect folks who buy your land to make a living if they don't get water?"

"I'm counting on Gardner building a system of ditches and reservoirs for us."

"Got any assurance he will?"

"Yes. If he likes the valley and the people."

Velie puffed a moment. "Well, Morgan, quite a few of us around here have had the same notion, but you're the first who has tried to do anything about it. Guess it's up to us to make your friend Gardner like the valley and the people."

The medico waited in the cave until it was dark. "Can't take chances on pulling out in daylight," he said. "If I know Broad, these mountains are crawling with Turkey Track men."

"Why didn't he find me?" Morgan asked.

Velie grinned. "Tell him, Jewell."

"This is my cave, Murdo. I come here lots of times just to get away from the valley. Sometimes I stay several days. There's water in the back of the cave and I always keep dry wood and some grub here. Dad just rode by, I guess."

Velie snorted. "I'll tell the rest of it, Morgan. Broad knew it was here, but Jewell, like a danged fool, gets up on top and starts a rock slide. That's why we had to move all them rocks when we got here."

"Doc, it wasn't as bad—" Jewell began.

"It was worse," Velie said testily. "You risked your fool neck to get them rocks to rolling. The reason Broad didn't look in here was because he saw the rock pile filling up the mouth of the cave. He figured that if you were inside, you'd be there a long time, so he rode on. Dunno what it is about you, Morgan, that makes women risk . . ." He stopped and cleared his throat. "Dunno what would make a levelheaded girl like Jewell risk her neck for you."

"It's the job he's got to do," Jewell said quickly.

"I reckon." Velie picked up his bag. "Stay here, Morgan. Savvy? You go to sashaying around and you'll open that bullet hole. Then there'll be hell to pay."

"I'll stay," Morgan said.

"All right. I'll be back in a few days. Take your medicine and behave yourself." He jerked his head at Jewell and she followed him to the mouth of the cave. He said in a low tone: "That stuff I gave him will knock him out for a day or two, but he won't be in any shape to fight for a long time. Broad will stick on his trail."

"I know," she said bitterly. "I've lived in Dad's house long enough to know what he'll do."

"He's a damned bulldog," Velie growled. "The only chance Morgan's got is for Broad to think he's dead. Might cash in, too. Lost enough blood to kill a couple of men. That bullet hole don't look real good, neither. He'll have a tough time if he works up a fever."

# Chapter 14: "Let the People Fight"

THE LONG NIGHT RIDE, THE MEMORY OF TOM Carrick's death that nagged him with useless regret, the loss of blood, and the shock of the wound itself all added up to more punishment than a man could take. Jewell, watching Morgan from across the fire, felt pity stir her. Murdo Morgan was a strong man, sure of himself and his own destiny. Now, remembering the square cut of his shoulders as he sat his saddle, his walk, the way he carried his gun, she felt the injustice of life in bringing this on him. What wrong had been committed was not of his doing.

Jewell threw wood on the fire and cooked another meal. Morgan sat up, shoulder blades against the rock wall of the cave, and tried to eat. He pushed the tin plate away, still half filled, and grinned wearily. "Got a flatiron in my stomach, I reckon."

She rolled a cigarette for him and put it into his mouth. "That will taste good," she said.

"Hell of a thing," he muttered. "Having you wait on me like I was a baby."

It was the first time, she guessed, that he had ever been laid up. He resented his weakness, resented being brought to the place where he had to have help. He had been a man who helped others, not the kind who received.

"I don't mind, Murdo," she said.

There was much of Broad Clancy's pride in her. It was that pride which kept her from thinking of him as much as she would have liked to. She was afraid to let her feelings go uncontrolled. When this job was done, he would drift on. She had to keep telling herself that. She was just a woman, who, by an accident of life, happened to be in position to help him. Probably there were a dozen like her along his back trail.

Morgan finished his cigarette, took one of the pills Doc Velie had left, and laid back. A moment later he was asleep, completely exhausted. Jewell sat up, staring into the slowly dying fire, playing with a discovery that had crept up on her, a discovery that even her pride could not keep her from recognizing. She was in love with Murdo Morgan.

She had never been in love before. Her life had been a lonely one, riding and thinking and living within herself, hating much of what she saw around her. She had spent hours in exactly this same place, never dreaming that she would be here again, looking after the man she loved. But with him or without him, win or lose, she loved him, and there would be no changing it, regardless of what was destined to happen.

Then, for no understandable reason, she

thought of Peg Royce, and a hot illogical anger filled her. There was always a stream of gossip in the valley, thin with human justice, thick with cruel malice. It was no secret that Buck Carrick was in love with Peg, that Rip liked her, and Jewell remembered hearing Broad tell the boy in no uncertain terms that he would not have a nester's girl in his family; she remembered Rip's flippant, "A man's got a right to have his fun," and Broad's understanding grin.

Rip would never have made the girl a husband, but Buck Carrick would. That thought lingered in Jewell's mind, feeding fuel to her anger. Peg should be satisfied with Buck. She remembered Velie's joking remark about not knowing what it was about Morgan that made women risk their necks for him. Velie had changed it quickly, but she had known what he'd meant. Rip had said he'd have shot Morgan the first day he was in the valley when Pete Royce jumped him from the back if Peg hadn't caught Rip's arm.

Then the anger washed out of Jewell. People judged Peg to be bad because she rode at night to keep her dates with men. By the same standards they would misjudge Jewell. No one would believe she rode at all hours and in all kinds of weather for as simple a reason as wanting to be by herself.

Whether Peg was good or bad was not as important as the depth of the girl's feeling for Morgan.

That, the way Jewell saw it, was something he would have to determine. He would do better to ride out of the valley alone than to be burdened with a woman who married him because he was the best she could do, or to show the valley that she had a better choice than Buck Carrick.

Then Jewell let a dream weave through her consciousness, a dream that was sweet and lingered in her mind with seductive promptings, of marriage to Murdo Morgan and a love that would make her life complete. She had seen hate from the day she had been old enough to recognize it; she knew what it did to people. Love was the only antidote for it. Then another thought burned through her mind, wiping out her dream. She was Broad Clancy's daughter! Viewing the future with cold logic, she could see but one end to all of it. Her father would kill Morgan, or Morgan would kill him.

She made her bed across the fire from Morgan, but sleep was an elusive thing. A sense of final futility built a gray discontent in her mind. She might save Morgan's life this time, but what of the next day, or week, or month? The night ribboned out and later she slept to wake with sunlight a red glory in the mouth of the cave.

Morgan regarded her with uncertain eyes. She saw, from his flushed face, that fever was upon him. He tried to get up and she let him try. He sank back, sweat breaking through the skin of his face. "No good," he muttered. "Just no damned good."

She cooked breakfast, but he found it hard to eat. He dropped off to sleep again, and she kept herself busy enlarging the hole at the mouth of the cave.

A chill feeling of despair grew in Jewell through the day. There seemed to be nothing she could do. Morgan was running a high temperature. He woke at times and called for her or mumbled something that was unintelligible and went back to sleep. She changed the dressing on his wound, and because there was nothing else to do, left the cave in search of wood.

Night then, and no sound but the stomping of their horses or the hooting of an owl or an occasional coyote call. In the morning Morgan's fever broke. He was pale and he looked tired. He tried to grin at Jewell as he said, "I'm beholden to you."

She wanted to cry. She wanted to kneel beside him and put her arms around him, to kiss him and tell him he owed her nothing. She had done what she had done freely and willingly. But she could do none of those things. There had been little show of affection in the Clancy family. Besides, she was not Peg Royce.

"If you do what you plan to do, Murdo," she said simply, "I'll be beholden to you."

She saw that he gave thought to what she had

said. He ate his breakfast with wolfish eagerness, and afterward asked her about it.

"It's hard to tell you," she said slowly. "It's just that I've talked to Abel Purdy and Doc Velie and some of the others. They're afraid of Dad. All but Doc. They want his business and his good will, but deep down, they hate him. Maybe because they're afraid of him. Or because they'd have a lot more business if settlers came into the valley. All of them say that hundreds of families could make a living here and that's the way it should be. I guess I've dreamed the same kind of dream you have, Murdo."

"Turkey Track doesn't mean to you what it does to Broad?"

"It doesn't mean anything at all. I . . . I guess I hate it. I've seen what he's done to others to make it what it is. It's become a sort of monster riding on his shoulders."

"You don't like a ranch?"

"I love everything about a ranch, but Turkey Track is an empire. Dad talks about the land company getting the wagon-road grant by fraud. I guess that's true, but it still doesn't belong to us. As long as Turkey Track is what it is now, settlers won't even occupy government land."

"Broad could have bought the quarter where his house is," Morgan mused. "By feeding his cattle and using the same summer range he does now, he could have hung on."

"I've talked to him about that, but he'd never consider it. He never settled for half of anything in his life."

Morgan held out his paper and tobacco sack and she rolled a cigarette for him. "Funny thing," he said. "I've done a little bit of everything, all the time thinking about a spread of my own. I like cattle. Like to handle 'em and see 'em grow, but when I had a stake, I took a long chance on this road grant. If I win, I'll have a real stake. If I lose, I'll be busted again."

"What will you do if you win?"

"Buy an outfit, I guess, or start one of my own somewhere. This is something I had to do. Hope Dad knows about it."

"Your father could see ahead," Jewell said bitterly. "Mine can't. He's like a European aristocrat. He thinks any change is bad."

"I've seen plenty of cowmen that way," Morgan said. "Change makes them lose. Even a railroad brings in settlers. If the cowmen keep the railroad out, the settlers can't get their stuff to market, but cows can walk to a railhead."

She was silent for a time, thinking about what he had said, and a little frightened by the future. Then her thoughts turned to her father and she could not help pitying him. With Rip dead, the foundation upon which Broad had built his life was gone.

"It isn't that Dad's dishonest," she said. "He

believes he's right in holding what he's fought for. He says the farmers always come after the cattlemen have tamed the country."

"Sure," Morgan said wearily, "but the country would have pretty slim picking if the farmers never got there."

She rose and moved to the mouth of the cave. "I'll get some wood." She paused, looking at him, deeply troubled. She said finally, "Don't judge all the Clancys the way you have to judge Dad."

"Why, I reckon I haven't."

She found little reassurance in his words. She left the cave, suddenly angry with herself. She had hoped he would say more, but she was not a woman who could put the words into a man's mouth she wanted to hear.

Velie came later in the week when they were outside the cave seeking the warmth of the afternoon sun.

"Tough as a bootheel, ain't you," the medico prodded. "A dose of lead can't even keep you down."

Morgan threw a glance at Jewell. "Not as tough as I figgered. I was aiming to start back to town, but she showed me different when she got the notion we ought to walk out here."

Velie laughed. "Tough gents like you never know when they're down. Let me tell you something, mister. You feel fine when you're lying on your back, but the first time you have a scrap you'll feel different."

"What are you driving at?"

"Let's have a look at you first." He nodded with satisfaction when he examined the wound. "Good as you could expect. Now it's a proposition of behaving yourself."

"What about this scrap?"

Velie pulled his pipe out of his pocket and dribbled tobacco into it. "You know how things stack up as well as I do. Royce and Blazer have been hanging around town, bragging about what they'll do to you when you show up. Broad got back last night after turning over every mushroom in the mountains looking for you. He figures Jewell is out looking, too, so he ain't real sure you've cashed in."

Jewell, knowing him well, saw what he was getting at. She said, "If I showed up in town and let on I couldn't find him, Dad would quit looking."

"That's the way I figure things." Velie blew a series of smoke rings. "He knows you've been over these hills more'n he has. If you can't find Morgan, he must be gone." He waggled a finger at Morgan. "Don't show up in town till the middle of August."

"The middle of August?" Morgan shouted. "Hell, Doc, there's a million things I've got to do before then."

Velie pulled his pipe out of his mouth, gaunt face scarred by worry. "Morgan, for once try using your head. This is more than your fight. It's a chance for a lot of people to get homes. If you lose, things don't change. If you win, this valley can be made into the paradise old Broad named it for. Go back now, and you'll be dead by morning. A man's got to be well to fight."

Morgan rubbed a stubble-dark cheek. Jewell, her eyes pinned on his face, sensed that he was trying to see it the way Velie did, trying to wait when his pride pressed him to go back. He said then: "I've got to see Jim. I let Tom get killed."

"You didn't let him get killed," Jewell said. "You had left the window open when it happened. Rip drew first. You thought they'd stall around until you got downstairs."

"I should have hollered from the window," Morgan muttered.

"It wouldn't have done any good, Murdo. Carrick would have looked up and Rip would have shot him. Or Flint would have got him in the back just like he did. They must have seen Carrick coming."

"They sure had him whipsawed." Morgan got up, restlessness thrusting at him, and sat down again. "I hadn't thought of it that way. You tell Jim, Doc."

"I'll tell him," Velie promised. "He wouldn't hold it against you anyhow." He nodded at

Jewell. "We'd better make dust. I came by Mossbrain's shack. He's sick, so I had an excuse for riding out this way, but I don't want anybody to start wondering why I stayed so long."

"Flint stole Mossbrain's horse," Morgan said.

Velie nodded. "Broke his leg in the lava. I found him and shot him."

Morgan drew some gold coins from his pocket and handed them to Velie. "See that Mossbrain gets a horse, Doc. I dunno about staying here. . . ."

"Damn it," Velie bawled. "I know how long it takes a man to get his strength back."

"But Gardner's got to know—" Morgan began.

"I wrote Gardner a letter," Velie cut in. "Told him what had happened and said he'd better get a move on getting here. Judging from that letter of his, I'd say he can do anything that needs to be done. Jim'll see the hay's hauled to town. Trouble with you, Morgan, is that you think this is your fight. It's more than that. Let the people do some of it."

Watching Morgan, Jewell saw him beat down his pride. When he looked at her there was a softness in his gray eyes. He said, "No way out of it. Maybe me and Broad are both wrong. But if it works out so Broad . . ."

He stopped, failing to find the words he wanted, but she knew what he meant. If Broad Clancy died at Morgan's hand, there would be a wall between them that nothing could break down, but she was not one to be blinded by her hopes and feelings. Morgan was terribly right when he said there was no way out of it. Nodding soberly, she said, "Do what you have to do, Murdo."

# Chapter 15: Clancy Beef for Nesters

MORGAN RODE BACK INTO IRISH BEND before the middle of August, the uncertainty of what was happening and the pressure of what had to be done driving him into action. His wound was healed, the soreness gone, and strength was back in his whip-muscled body. Yet there was a difference in him that went deeper than the beard covering his face and the hungry leanness that gave his features a mild resemblance to those of a brooding hawk.

He was a forward-looking man, never one to waste time in regrets. Still, Tom Carrick's death weighed heavily upon him, a weight that the killing of Jaggers Flint had not removed.

Racking his black in front of the barbershop, Morgan had a shave and haircut and sent the barber to the store for a new shirt while he had a bath. He was not certain whether the barber knew him or not, but as the man was coolly distant, he thought he had been recognized. He remembered the hostility he had felt the first day he was here. It was no different now, and it wouldn't be until they saw that Clancy was beaten. Then Murdo Morgan would have friends, dozens of them.

Morgan was leaning back in the zinc tub

lathering his long body when he heard steps cross the barbershop toward the back room. The word was out that he was in town. He had left his gun belt over a chair within easy reach, an instinctive precaution that he had taken without thought. He lifted his Colt from holster, soapy thumb slipping on the heavy hammer as he tried to cock the gun. He cursed, wiped his hand on the towel, and had the hammer pronged back when the door opened. It was Doc Velie and Grant Gardner.

"Hell of a note when a man can't take a bath without being busted in on, ain't it?" Velie asked complacently.

Gardner paused in the doorway, suddenly embarrassed as if, in his anxiety to see Morgan, he had not thought how it would be. Morgan grinned. "Howdy, Doc." Letting down the hammer, he laid his gun on the chair and held out a wet hand. "Howdy, Gardner."

"Hell of a note when a man greets his friends with a cocked gun, too," Velie complained. "Ain't it, Gardner?"

"From what I've seen since I got to Paradise Valley," Gardner said soberly, "I'd say it was a good idea to greet anybody with a gun until you know who it is."

Morgan laid his gaze on the capitalist's face. "What happened?"

"Nothing," Velie said quickly. "Broad decided

you're dead. Jewell had a row with him and moved to the hotel, but he's got a man watching her. That's why she didn't come out to see you."

Gardner lifted a cigar from his pocket. "I'm used to situations like this. Fact is, I had to do a little fighting on my own hook when I started carving up a cowman's range." He fished in his pocket for a match. "But this one's the toughest deal I've been on. You're still on top, but a man's luck doesn't last forever."

"A man makes his own luck," Morgan said. "I'll make mine. Like you said in your letter. My job is to keep the peace."

"And a tough job it is with most of it still ahead of you," Gardner murmured. "Mine's about finished. Every contract's been sold. Next week we'll put up the big tent and we'll have a field kitchen for the settlers who aren't equipped to cook their own meals. The hotel is far from adequate, so we'll have to put up another tent for them to sleep in."

"Springs and mattresses, I reckon," Velie grunted.

Gardner waited until he had his cigar going. "Hay on the ground, and they'll be damned glad to get it. There is another problem, Morgan. Whenever you get a crowd like we're going to have, you get a number of grifters and gamblers who have to be handled. I have a feeling you'll be busy without taking care of the riffraff."

189

"There's a lawman here named Purdy," Morgan said.

Velie snorted. "Don't figger on Purdy."

"A little confidence might go a long ways with him," Morgan murmured.

"Purdy thinks too much," Velie growled. "Reading and thinking don't give a man guts. Confidence don't either."

"We'll try him," Morgan said sharply.

"That's up to you," Gardner said doubtfully. "The barber's back, Doc. We'd better let the man dress."

"Nothing's stopping him," Velie snapped. He slid exploratory fingers over Morgan's shoulder. "Don't get the idea we came in here because we were so damned glad to see you. Just professional interest. H'm. I did a good job on you. Healed up fine. Surprisin', considering you had to eat your own cooking after Jewell left."

"I didn't stay there. Rode over to Prineville. Then spent some time on the Deschutes."

"Couldn't stay put, could you?" Velie's eyes smoldered with anger. "Well, now that you're back, see if you can stay alive. Blazer and Royce have been hanging around the Elite. Talking about what they'll do to you if you show up. They never did take to the yarn that Flint tagged you and you'd crawled off to die."

Morgan got out of the tub and reached for the towel. "See you later."

Gardner left the room but Velie paused in the doorway, eyes speculatively on Morgan.

"Shut the door," Morgan howled.

"Hell, you're not so pretty," the medico grunted. "I told you Jewell's at the hotel."

"I heard you. Shut the door."

Growling something that didn't reach Morgan as words, Velie slammed the door and left the barbershop.

Morgan dressed and buckled on his gun belt, thinking with grim reluctance that Gardner had been right in saying the job of keeping the peace was a tough one and most of it was still ahead. He wondered how accurate Velie had been in his harsh judgment of Purdy. If the medico was right, he was wrong, but if Purdy had even a small part of a man's natural heritage of pride, he was right and Velie was wrong. He'd have to know before the crowd came.

Leaving the barbershop, Morgan paced along the front of the saddlery, eyes on the street. It was nearly as deserted as it had been the day he had seen Abel Purdy, but an apparently deserted town could be a dangerous one. Both Royce and Blazer, like Jaggers Flint had been, were the kind who would shoot him from a hiding place if they thought the law was too weak to handle them.

By this time the news of Morgan's presence would have swept the town like a prairie fire before a high wind. Pausing in front of the hotel,

Morgan remembered there had been two horses racked before the Elite when he rode into town. Now the hitch pole was empty. He turned into the lobby, pondering this, but failing to see any danger in it.

Jewell`was not behind the desk. Disappointment built a gray uneasiness in him. He had not realized until he swung into the dining room how much he had counted on seeing her. When he had eaten, he asked for her at the desk.

The clerk eyed him with the same veiled hostility he had sensed in the barber. "She ain't here, mister. Out riding, I reckon."

Morgan wheeled out of the lobby. He made a smoke as he moved along the walk to the corner, stopped in front of the Stockmen's Bank and scratching a match across its front, lighted his cigarette. He stood there, considering, tobacco smoke a shifting shape in front of his face. As long as Blazer and Royce were in town, they were as dangerous as a pair of rattlesnakes in a man's bed.

Decision made, Morgan slanted across the intersection to the store, gaze fixed on the front of the Elite. He had to kill Blazer and Royce or drive them out of the valley. Both claimed to be settlers, and for that reason were capable of doing irreparable damage when the contract holders arrived in Irish Bend.

It wasn't until Morgan reached the post office

that he saw the newly lettered sign hanging in front of what had been an empty building east of the Elite: OFFICE OF CASCADE & PARADISE LAND COMPANY. He grinned as he turned into Purdy's place. Gardner, he thought, was a good man to be running things.

Purdy blinked behind his spectacles. Then he rose and gravely held out his hand. "Greetings from a mortal to one in the other world. I understand you're dead with Flint's bullet in you."

"It's a lie. The slug went on through."

Purdy laughed and motioned to a chair. "Sit down, Morgan. I'm glad to see you."

Morgan shook his head. "I've got business in the Elite. I hear Royce and Blazer are all set for me."

"They've done some wild talking," Purdy admitted.

"I'm giving 'em a chance to show how much is wind, which same brings up another point. Gardner says we'll have some toughs in town when the crowd gets in. Are you going to handle them?"

It was a blunt question, brutally put. Purdy looked down at his star, holding his answer for a moment. He was afraid. Morgan saw that in the sudden squeeze fear put upon his features, but instinct did not force a quick refusal from him. His pride, then, was not dead, and Morgan knew his confidence had not been wasted.

"I'll try," Purdy said at last.

"Good." Morgan nodded as if there had never been any doubt. He lifted his gun, checked it, and slid it back into leather. "Come on over to the Elite. Might as well see the fun."

Purdy hesitated, then turned to his desk, and picking up an ancient Navy Colt, slipped it into his waistband. He said, "I wouldn't want to miss it."

They angled across the dust strip toward the Elite. Doc Velie, coming out of the company office, stared in the way of a man who sees something unreal take the cloak of reality.

They reached the walk, crossed it, and Morgan said: "I just want a fair fight. See that I get it." He put a shoulder against the batwings and pushed through, hand on gun butt. Except for the droopy-mouthed barman, the place was empty, but hoof thunder sounded from the alley and faded as distance grew.

"They're not here," Purdy said, as if this evident fact was something he had hoped for but had not expected.

Morgan moved directly to the bar. "Where's Royce and Blazer?"

The barman laid down his towel. "Dunno. They went out of the back door when you two left Purdy's office. Reckon they've made some dust by now."

"I've been in town two hours," Morgan said.

"How come they got in such a hurry all of a sudden?"

"They knowed you was here," the barman said. "They aimed to gun you down the minute you showed your nose in the door, but they got another notion when they saw Purdy. Funny how a star can change a man's mind."

Morgan grinned at the astounded Purdy. The pale-eyed man had discovered something new concerning the dignity of a lawman's badge.

"We'd better have a drink on that, Abel," Morgan said. "I'm a little put out. I figgered it was me that had them hombres worried."

"You did." The barman set a bottle and glasses on the mahogany. "That was why they weren't taking any chances on you, but they didn't figger on the law, so they got spooked when they saw Purdy."

Morgan took his drink and jingled a coin on the bar. "See you later, Abel," he said, and left the saloon.

The building that housed the company's office had been a store, but the owner had lost an argument to Broad Clancy and left the valley. It had been filled with broken chairs and boxes, a long counter, dirt, and innumerable cobwebs. Morgan paused in the doorway, amazed by what he saw. The place was clean, the debris cleared out, and the smell of fresh paint lingered in the air. There were several desks in the front of the room behind a railing that was a line of demarcation between the clerical workers and a waiting room for visitors. Two small office rooms had been built in the back, one lettered Grant Gardner, the other, Murdo Morgan.

Gardner saw Morgan and bustled out of his office. "Been watching for you. I wanted you to see what we've done."

"Looks fine," Morgan murmured. "Never thought I'd have my name on an office door."

Gardner flushed with evident pleasure. "This is part of my contribution to a worthwhile endeavor, Morgan." He pointed to a row of filing cabinets along the wall. "Duplicate copies of the contracts that have been sold. My office crew will be in from Alturas tomorrow. Lot of work yet for all of us. I want you to go over a map of the road grant with me. We'll mark off the tracts according to the size you want them sold. All this bookkeeping and the cost of taking care of our customers and the traveling expenses for those who represent twenty or more contracts will cut into your profit, but in the long run it will pay."

Gardner swung his hand around the room. "Show stuff, maybe, but it impresses folks. A lot of them will want to come in and talk and we'll have to take time off. If we can keep them in good humor and hold their confidence, the drawing will go off like clockwork." He opened the door into Morgan's office. "How do you like that?"

A new swivel chair, rolltop desk, brass spittoon on the floor, three chairs. Sitting down at his desk, Morgan ran his finger tips across the varnished wood. "Well," he whispered, "I'll be damned."

Gardner began fishing for a cigar. "A few more things to tell you," he said casually. "This valley is far superior to what I had expected to see. Jim Carrick tells me that the soil is good and the water is here if reservoirs are built to hold it. I intend to do that if the settlers are the solid citizens my salesmen say they are. Back there they've been blowed out, dried out, burned out, and starved out. They're looking for a place where there is water, good soil, and a moderate climate."

Morgan leaned back in his chair, boots on the desk top. "We've got them things," he said, and waited.

Gardner bit off the end of his cigar and dug into his pocket for a match. "Folks like a show. We're selling land and after that I'll sell them water. I've got a surveying crew in the hills now. We've got to live with them, so we want to start off right. The thing we've got to avoid is to let them get any idea that the drawing is crooked. Knowing Ed Cole, I'm damned sure he'll work on that end."

Gardner found a match and striking it, fired his cigar. Still Morgan held his silence, knowing from Gardner's roundabout approach that there was more to come.

"I've been pounding my brain until I got the right idea." Gardner blew out a long smoke plume. "Pretty girls always appeal to a crowd of men, so I want you to line up two pretty girls to help with the drawing."

This was what Gardner had been working up to. Morgan took his feet off the desk and stood up. Jewell Clancy and Peg Royce were the only pretty girls in the valley as far as he knew, and he couldn't ask either one.

"I won't do it," Morgan said angrily. "Peg's dad is Pete Royce and Jewell's is Broad Clancy. You know how both of them stand."

Gardner waved his cigar at Morgan. "That's the reason we want them. The settlers can't accuse us of being crooked with those girls doing the drawing."

"I won't do it," Morgan said hotly. "You're crazy to think I would."

Gardner's chubby face reddened. "I was crazy to contract with the Sneed boys to butcher wild hogs so we'd have pork for our customers. I was crazy to ride out to Broad Clancy's camp and ask him for beef. I suppose I was crazy to come up here . . ."

"What the hell are you talking about?"

"We contracted to furnish water, fresh meat, and horse feed during the drawing and for a week

198

before to those who get here early. I heard that there were wild hogs in the tules, so I got the Sneed boys to butcher enough to keep us in fresh meat until we get Clancy's beef to the settlers."

"You asked Broad Clancy to furnish us with fresh meat?" Morgan demanded.

"Why not?"

"Nothing, except it don't make sense for him to do it. I can't understand why he didn't pull a gun on you when you went up there."

"He was very courteous," Gardner said stiffly. "Abel Purdy went with me. He introduced us and the instant I told Clancy what I wanted he said he'd sell us all we needed. I told him we'd pay top price and save him a drive to the railhead."

"It don't make sense," Morgan said stubbornly. "You don't know Clancy. He was ornery before Rip was killed. He'll be twice as bad now."

"You've got him wrong," Gardner argued. "He sees the handwriting on the wall and he's smart enough to read it."

Morgan let it go at that, but he knew Clancy wasn't a man to look for handwriting on the wall. He'd use his beef as a lethal weapon to wreck the land sale, and there was no way to counter his move unless Morgan could find out what it was.

Gardner fidgeted at the door, puffing fiercely on his cigar and eyeing Morgan. Finally he said: "I didn't think you'd get your neck bowed over asking those girls to help. We've got to figure every corner and it's my guess hell will pop in a few days. I've already told them you'd ask them."

So he was committed. He said, "All right," and sat down at his desk again, feet cocked in front of him. He didn't notice when Gardner left. Resentment died in him. Gardner was a good man with savvy for his part of the business, the kind of savvy Morgan didn't have, but Gardner lacked the understanding Morgan had about men like Broad Clancy. Hell would pop all right, and probably over Turkey Track beef.

# Chapter 16: Woman Against Woman

MORGAN WAS STILL AT HIS DESK WHEN THE rumble of a heavily loaded wagon brought him to the street door. Jim Carrick was bringing in another load of hay, Buck lying on his back behind him, hat pulled over his face.

Morgan hesitated, knowing this was something that had to be done. He should have ridden out to Carrick's place. He went back for his hat, and when he reached the street Carrick had turned at the intersection and pulled in behind the Silver Spur saloon.

The wagon was stopped beside a half-formed stack when Morgan reached it. He called, "Howdy, Jim."

Carrick stepped away from the load, saw who it was, and let out a squall. "Well, damn me if it ain't Murdo. Where you been, boy?"

Morgan gripped the farmer's hard hand. His fear had been groundless. Jim Carrick held no bitterness toward him. "Getting over a bullet hole Flint gave me."

"Doc said you'd been shot to hell, but I couldn't keep from thinking you'd be back, so I went ahead on this hay deal. Gardner took over and that's what he said to do."

"That's right." Morgan swung a hand toward the finished stacks. "There's a lot of hay. I don't have any idea if we'll use all of it."

"Better have it on hand. Tried to buy some of Royce's old hay, but hell, he wouldn't let it go."

"We'll have enough. Some of the settlers will come by stage or horseback. Soon as the drawing's over the majority of 'em will scatter and figger on coming back in the spring."

"Buck's up on the load," Carrick said as if suddenly remembering. "Buck, Murdo's here."

Young Carrick shoved his face into view, dislike stamped upon it. "Yeah, I heard him. Kept hoping you'd cashed in, Morgan."

Jim's eyes hardened. "You're too old and too big to have to lick, but I'll do it if I hear any more of that out of you."

Buck grunted an oath and drew back.

"He's still in love," Morgan murmured.

"Don't make no difference," Carrick said bitterly. "He's been seeing that Royce girl. She came over a time or two after you left. Soon as he could stay in a saddle he rode over there, but she won't marry him."

" 'Bout Tom." Morgan dug a boot toe into the dirt. "I was there when he was killed. Maybe there was some way I could have—"

"None of that talk," Carrick said sharply. "Doc told me how it was. I talked to the Clancy girl, too. Tom just had to keep looking for trouble till he found it. Headed for town soon as he got back the day you left. Allowed there'd be fighting and he was gonna side you."

"If I'd known that, I'd have talked to him," Morgan said. "Maybe he'd have stayed in town."

"No sense blaming yourself. You plugged Flint and got yourself shot up to boot. What's done is done. I ain't seen old Broad since it happened, but they tell me he's 'bout loco. Keep your eyes on him, son." Carrick paused, gaze on somebody behind Morgan. He muttered, "There she is."

"Murdo, I heard you were back."

It was Peg Royce, panting with her run, dark eyes afire with pleasure. Morgan started to say something, but didn't, for Peg threw her arms around his neck and pulled his lips down to hers.

There was no reserve about her, no holding back, no subterfuge. She had never made any secret of her want of him, and now she told the world. Even then, with the sweet taste of her lips upon his, with the heat of her kiss burning through him, the thought of Jewell Clancy was a quick repelling force in his mind.

"All right." Buck Carrick slid off the load to the ground.

Peg stepped away from Morgan, composed and unabashed. "Hello, Buck. I told you the bullet hadn't been molded that could kill him."

"I wish to hell it'd been me instead of Flint that had that chance." Buck took another step toward

Morgan, great shoulders hunched, fists balled in front of him, handsome face turned ugly by the fury of his rage. "I'm gonna bust you, Morgan. If I had a gun, I'd kill you."

Indecision gripped Morgan. He stepped back, thinking of Tom Carrick, of Jim and how much he owed him, and knew he couldn't fight Buck. He said: "Don't try it. I've got nothing to fight you for."

Buck's laugh was a taunting slap. "I sure as hell have got something to fight you for."

"Which same don't make a girl love you," Morgan said.

He went back another step, heard Peg cry: "Don't, Buck. If you love me, don't," but Buck didn't stop. Weeks of smoldering hate exploded in him now, taking him beyond the edge of reason.

"You was sweet on her all the time," Buck bawled. "I ain't been fooled a little bit. She'd of married me this summer if it hadn't been for you. Now I'm gonna fix that mug of yours so she won't do no more kissing on it."

A great fist swung out. He had strength, nothing more, and Morgan knew he could cut him down with half a dozen driving blows. Still he couldn't do it. He ducked the fist and retreated, still searching for something that would stop the boy. Peg was at Buck's side, beating at him with her fists, crying: "He doesn't want to fight you, you fool. I'd never marry you. I never would have."

It was Jim Carrick who stopped it. Gripping his pitchfork, the tines shining in the sunlight, he brought it forward in a quick jab, stabbing Buck in the rump. Buck let out a howl of pain and throwing his shoulders back in an involuntary motion, grabbed his seat.

"Git back on that load," Jim said hoarsely. "If I have to do that again, you'll be eating off a high shelf for the rest of the summer."

Buck sidled toward the wagon, fight gone out of him, but the bitterness was still there, a hatred that would fester with time until he became a madman capable of murder. Without a word, he climbed back on the load.

Peg gripped Morgan's arm. "I want to talk to you," she whispered.

Nodding at Jim Carrick, Morgan turned away, deeply troubled. He respected and liked Carrick as he had respected and liked few men. He would be largely indebted to him for whatever success he had with the land sale, but life was dealing off the bottom of the deck. First he had been indirectly to blame for Tom's death. Now Buck was working himself into a killing frenzy.

"I've been looking for you," Peg said hurriedly. "Every time I came to town, I asked Gardner. Why didn't you let me know?"

"I didn't think you'd worry. Doc thought it was better if nobody knew."

"You knew I'd worry," she said hotly. Then

bitterness touched her face. "You were right. Pete Royce is my father. I couldn't be trusted."

"It wasn't that. No one knew."

They rounded the Silver Spur and went on across the street. Peg said, as if she had only then thought of it: "Let's have supper in the hotel, Murdo. Royce hasn't been home for a long time, and I'm tired of eating alone."

Murdo grunted, "All right," not wanting to, because he hadn't seen Jewell and he didn't want to meet her with Peg on his arm. But if Peg felt his lack of enthusiasm, she gave no indication of it.

"Royce and Blazer are hanging around to kill you," she said, "if you turned up alive. Cole will be here for the drawing. I wanted to tell you about him the last time, but I couldn't. You thought he was your friend . . ."

"I know. He saw Broad Clancy. Jewell told me what he was trying to do."

"Jewell told—" She bit her lip, not letting her sudden flare of anger show. "What are you going to do when he comes back?"

They reached the hotel and went in. "I don't know," Morgan said. He had known it was a situation he would have to face. Cole would come back to see if Murdo Morgan had been destroyed, and Morgan honestly didn't know what would happen then. He shrank, even in his thoughts, from killing this man he had called friend.

"It's good to see you on your feet, Murdo."

It was Jewell, coming down the stairs beyond the desk. She was wearing a blue bombazine dress with long sleeves. Morgan had not seen her in that dress before, and his eyes, taking in her small trim figure, showed his appreciation. He lifted his hat. "It's good to be on my feet."

Jewell nodded at Peg. "How are you, Peg?"

For an instant Peg made no answer. She stood tall and straight beside Morgan, hand still possessively on his arm, her head high, pointed breasts rising and falling with her breathing as she fought for self-control. Morgan, turning his gaze to her, saw the pulse beat in her throat, the quiver of her lips. She had, he guessed, sought this meeting, and now that it was here, she couldn't bring it off the way she had planned.

"I'm fine, Jewell," Peg said. "We're having supper. Won't you come with us?"

"Thank you, but I've had supper."

"Gardner said he'd told you girls I'd ask you to help with the drawing," Morgan said bluntly. "That ain't just right, knowing how your—"

"I'll be glad to," Peg said quickly.

Jewell hesitated, and she was the one about whom Morgan was most concerned. Pete Royce was no good. Everybody in the valley knew that. Peg hated him, and she would help with the drawing to spite him, if for no other reason. Broad Clancy was something else. Morgan knew

Jewell didn't agree with him, but she didn't hate him. He said: "Broad won't like it. Don't feel . . ."

"It's the least she can do, Murdo," Peg breathed. "Gardner said it would be a big help to you, because everybody would know it was an honest draw."

A smile touched Jewell's lips. "Of course I'll help, Murdo."

Peg's answering smile was quick and lip-deep. "I thought you would."

Morgan, looking from one to the other, did not fully understand. He only knew they were women, facing each other, fighting with claw instead of fist, one tall and dark and full-bodied, the other small and slim, with wheat-gold hair afire now with a slanted ray of sunlight falling across her head. There was this moment of tension, spark filled. It was steel pressed against a whirling emery wheel, and Morgan, striving desperately to find something to say to break the tension, could do no better than, "Doc says it healed up fine."

Jewell brought her eyes to Morgan. "I've worried about you. You were so weak when I left you."

Morgan felt Peg stiffen. She asked coldly, "You were with him when he was shot?"

"No, but I found him afterward. I guessed Flint would head for the lava flow and I was close enough to hear the shots. I stayed with Murdo until after his fever broke."

"And you left him when he was still weak?"

"Doc thought I should."

Peg's breath was a long sigh. She whispered: "If I was taking care of him, I'd have stayed until he was well."

"He should have sent for you," Jewell murmured.

"I was all right," Morgan cut in.

A sob came out of Peg, startlingly sudden. "You wouldn't send for me, would you, Murdo? You couldn't trust me like you could her."

She whirled out of the lobby and ran on through the dust of the street to her horse. Mounting, she quit town at a reckless pace.

"I'm sorry," Jewell said contritely. "I shouldn't have done it. I don't know why I did."

Still Morgan did not fully understand it. He only knew that women clash in a different way than men, that Jewell had struck back in self-defense. He turned toward the dining room, then swung back to say, "I don't want to bust you and your father up."

"You won't. I've already left home. Now go get your supper."

# Chapter 17: The Man Called Friend

GARDNER HAD FIGURED THE UNCERTAIN element of time as accurately as a man could. His office crew came north on the stage from Alturas, fast wagons bringing their equipment. Empty water wagons creaked across the desert to make the long haul from the streams around Clancy Mountain, where the water ran clear and cold in a swift lacy pattern. Lumbering freighters, starting earlier, brought food supplies, blankets, a heavy stove for the restaurant, tents, and lumber from Lakeview for the platform in the big tent and tables and benches for the dining room.

Morgan, watching idly because there was nothing for him to do at the moment, marveled at the military precision with which Gardner's men worked. Saws bit through pine. The ring of hammer on nail was a constant jangle of noise. Canvas was stretched, stakes pounded deep into the earth, ropes tightened. Within a matter of hours, Irish Bend had reached out across the flat to triple in size.

Gardner, flushing with pride, slapped Morgan on the back. "We're ready. Let them come." He grinned in sudden embarrassment. "You know, Morgan, I've kicked myself for not taking a partnership in this deal. I misjudged the land and I misjudged you. I thought the valley was too far from a railroad and I didn't believe you could take care of yourself against the opposition you'd have."

"We're a long ways from a railroad, and there's still plenty of opposition."

"Steel will come," Gardner said confidently. "And as for the opposition, Cole hasn't showed his face, Blazer and Royce have stayed out of town since you called their bluff, and looks like Clancy is convinced we mean business."

Gardner might be right about the railroad, but he was dead wrong on the opposition. Morgan's mind turned to Clancy's beef agreement, as it had continually during his waking hours since he had heard about it. The deal had been made. There was nothing to do but let time bring Clancy into the open.

"I couldn't have put this over if you hadn't given me a hand," Morgan said. "I didn't have no idea there would be all this whoop-dedoo when I bought the grant."

Gardner showed his pleasure. "Glad to do it, Morgan. Fact is, I'll be a partner when I get the ditch system in. Funny about me. Some men get their pleasure out of whisky or women. Bringing farmers onto good land where they can own their own home is mine." He chuckled. "Only this time somebody else is taking the risk. If the sale doesn't go off, you'll lose your shirt. If it does, you'll be a rich man."

"If it doesn't go off," Morgan said grimly, "you'll be digging into your pocket because my shirt won't pay for all this."

Gardner took a fresh grip on his cigar. "Guess we'd better see it goes over." He squinted up at the bright sky. "If the good weather holds like it has, we won't need to worry. We've taken care of everything but the weather, which is one thing you just have to leave to Providence."

They did come. By stage. By horseback. By buggies. By buckboards. And in covered wagons loaded with household goods, ready to stay through the winter, echoes of their passage singing across the sage and bunchgrass flat to die among the empty miles. All roads led to Irish Bend. There the trail ended, the human tide piled up, and chaos had to be hammered into order.

It was the same drama that had been enacted and reenacted through the centuries, the drama that had made America. Explorers driven on by the deathless urge to see beyond the skyline, to see where the rivers were born. Missionaries, men of God, their Bibles under their arms, risking their scalps to tell the howling blood-lusting brownskins about another world and their souls' salvation. Mountain men, buckskin clad, fringe a-sway, Indian wives and half-breed children, taking the savage's way of life, the savage driven into the empty land of the great silence because a stranger had built within sight of him, the smoke from his chimney corrupting the horizon.

Miners and prospectors, haunting the bars and gulches, urged on by an inner hunger for the yellow metal, building boom town after boom town, climbing above timber line where ten times out of nine, they said, you'd find silver. Cattlemen, land pirates, harking back to the feudal days of chivalry with the chivalry so often missing, hiring the knights of horse and rope and gun, an aristocracy taking what it wanted without a by-your-leave of anyone, holding to what they claimed by any means they had, surrendering only to death or the tidal wave of those whose best weapon was the plow.

With every wave there were the others: hangers-on, tradesmen, lawyers and doctors, preachers and teachers, blacksmiths and carpenters. Women, the virtuous and the tinseled, those who followed their men because theirs was a love and devotion that went beyond human analysis, those who merely followed men, accepting their sordid profession by choice or perhaps driven to it by the exigencies of life.

Bad men and good, outlaws and law-abiding, the strong who shaped life and the weak who were shaped by that life. Bunco artists. Grifters. Con men. All of them were here in Irish Bend, and Abel Purdy grew with the needs of the day.

Three men tried to hold up the Stockmen's Bank. Purdy caught them from one side, Morgan from the other, and the three of them died in the deep dust of Irish Bend's street while gunfire racketed between the paintless false fronts. A shell-game operator set up his board in front of the Silver Spur. Purdy invited him to leave. The invitation was accepted. A drunk accosted Jewell Clancy on the street. Morgan rammed his way through the crowd and knocked the man down. He spit out a tooth, wiped blood from his mouth, and bawled: "You own the town maybe, but you don't own the women." Morgan hauled him to his feet, knocked another tooth loose, and told him to leave town. Invitation again accepted.

It was rough and tough and turbulent, but Abel Purdy and Murdo Morgan held down the lid, and some of the turbulence died. Good men, these farmers. Driven by land hunger and a dream. Freckle-faced kids. Sunbonneted women. Weather-darkened men with hands curled to fit the handles of their plows. Kansans and Nebraskans and east-to-the-Appalachians.

"Good men," Gardner said. "That's why I'm aiming to build your irrigation system."

Good men, Morgan knew. Men with enough money to buy their land and still have some left for the hard years ahead. The raggle taggle, the visionary, the seekers of something for nothing would come later to settle on free government land. Maybe they would prove up. Maybe not. But these men were different. They would give the land a fair trial. If it beat them, they'd lose the stake they had spent half a lifetime making. If they lost, they'd move on and start again.

Jewell's hotel and Gardner's tent with its hay beds were filled. The store sold out and the owner cursed bitterly because he had lacked faith and failed to build up his stock. The hotel dining room seldom had an empty table and the tent restaurant did as well. At night campfires were stars stretching across the flat to the south of town. The haystacks the Carricks had built melted like snowdrifts before a burning sun. Kansas men gathered together. Nebraska men. Iowa. Missouri. Illinois. Visited and dreamed and stared at Clancy Mountain and allowed there might be deer up there.

In every group leaders lifted their heads above the others, were listened and toadied to and grew deep-chested with attention. Clay Daeton, from the Nebraska sand hills, shook Morgan's hand with respect. He turned his head and spat a brown ribbon that plopped into the wheel- and hoof-churned dust of the street. "Never seen a purtier valley, Mr. Morgan. Had some misgivings, coming so far on the big gab of men you sent out to sell your land. Figgered it might be just another rush, aiming to take the bark off our backs, but I reckon if you give us a fair sale next week, we'll be mighty well satisfied."

Good men. Excited a little by the crowd and a new land. Everything new. Talked to the old settlers like Jim Carrick. Asked him this and that. What were the winters like? Were the summers always this cool? What could you raise? Would fruit grow here? Satisfied, solid men riding out over the valley, scratching boot toes through the dirt, picking up a handful and letting it dribble between their fingers, finding the spots they hoped to draw.

Overnight old sleepy Irish Bend the cowtown was gone. A new Irish Bend, throbbing with boom-town life, more canvas than wood, mushroomed among the clumps of sage and rabbit brush. The old inhabitants scratched their heads and rubbed their eyes, and could not believe this thing they saw. Some cursed Murdo Morgan. Some looked at him with new interest and admitted that maybe Broad Clancy was finished. He hadn't showed up. He hadn't turned a hair. By this time he knew that Murdo Morgan was alive and in Irish Bend. It wasn't like Broad Clancy, and nobody understood. Not even Jewell. Not even Murdo Morgan. Then Ed Cole rode in from Prineville.

Morgan was in his office visiting with Clay Dalton and his Nebraska friends when his door opened. Gardner said, "Ed Cole's here."

Morgan rose, a pressure on his chest making

216

it hard to breathe. He said, "I'll go see what he wants."

He stepped into the main office, the clattering typewriters annoying him. He strode into Gardner's office, gritting his teeth against the clamor. Ed Cole was standing at the corner of Gardner's desk, an easy smile on his lips, blue eyes as guileless as they had been the day he'd sat in his San Francisco office and told Morgan he'd see about the loan.

"How are you, friend Murdo?" Cole said in a soft courteous voice. He held out his hand. "I came to watch the drawing. Looks like it'll be quite a show."

Gardner stepped in behind Morgan, closing the door after him. Morgan ignored Cole's hand. His breathing sawed into the quiet, air coming from the bottom of his lungs as he fought his anger. He said, "That ain't the reason you're here."

Cole dropped his hand, the mask of courtesy stripped from his face. He said harshly, "This is a hell of a way to greet a friend."

"Friend?" Morgan turned to Gardner. "Wonder what he'd say an enemy was."

Cole slipped his hands into his coat pockets. He might have a gun there. Morgan wasn't sure. Cole said: "Let's have it, Morgan. We've known each other a long time. You wouldn't be where you are now if I hadn't negotiated your loan for you."

"I ain't sure o' that, but what you said about knowing each other is right. I'm remembering the time them miners had you cornered in Ouray. They claimed you'd crooked 'em in a poker game. I didn't believe it then, but I do now. You were mighty glad I was around."

Cole licked dry lips. "Sure, Murdo. I returned the favor by helping you get a loan. Now, why the hell—"

"No use lying 'bout it, Ed. You got me the loan because you thought I was a cinch to lose out in this land sale and your bank would get the wagon-road grant for the price of the loan you'd made me. A damned steal, which makes you a robber same as if you'd held a gun on me."

Color bloomed in Cole's cheeks. He chewed a lip, eyes not so guileless now, as they whipped to Gardner and back to Morgan. Suddenly he was afraid. Morgan remembered the way he'd looked that night in Ouray. He saw the man now as he was, handsome and smooth mannered, but with neither love nor respect for anything or anybody but himself. He was like a tree covered by sound bark but utterly rotten inside.

"Who's been lying to you?" Cole asked in a vain attempt to bluff it through.

"Nobody. Jewell Clancy told me about you being out there to see Broad. You made a deal with him. If something went wrong and your back-shooting gundogs didn't get me, Broad was supposed to do the job and you were going to deed him the land he needed when your bank got the road grant. You never intended to keep that bargain, did you, Ed?"

"You've been lied to," Cole shouted.

"Then why did you come to the valley after I got here?" Morgan demanded. "If you were on the level, why didn't you see me? You're doing the lying, Ed. You put Blazer and Royce on my tail. Then you tried to make it a sure thing by seeing Clancy. Peg Royce said—"

"Peg wouldn't say anything. She took my money—" Cole caught himself. It was admission enough. Dull red crept over his face and on around to the back of his neck. There was this moment of struggle within him before he made a futile effort to keep his self-respect. He raged, "I'm not going to stand here and be called a liar."

Cole started for the door. Morgan grabbed a handful of his shirt and jerked him to a stop. "Coming here was your idea. Now you can answer a question. Why did Broad agree to sell us beef?"

"I don't know." Cole tried to pull free. "I haven't seen Broad."

Morgan shook him. "You paid Royce and Blazer to kill me, didn't you?"

Cole struck at Morgan, fist stinging his cheek. Morgan hit him, a wicked right that slammed Cole against the wall. He wiped a sleeve across a bloody nose, then his hand dropped to his pocket and he pulled a gun. Morgan jumped at him, gripping Cole's right wrist with his left hand, twisting until Cole dropped the gun. He kept on twisting, bringing Cole's body around until he cried out in agony. He kicked at Morgan, tried to hit him with his left.

Morgan said, "If I didn't make myself clear, I will now." He hit Cole again, driving him back to the wall. Cursing, Cole lowered his head and drove at him. Made wild by fear and pain, Cole forgot anything he had ever known about fighting. He tried to stomp on Morgan's toes. Drove a thumb at Morgan's eye. Lifted a knee to get him in the crotch. Nothing worked. Morgan was nowhere and everywhere, letting Cole's charge wear itself out.

When the wild fury in Cole had blunted itself on the hard rock of failure, Morgan sledged him on the point of the chin. Cole dropped his hands and shook his head. Then his knees gave and he fell. The door to Gardner's office had been opened. Clay Dalton and his Nebraska friends stood knotted there. Dalton called: "Boot him, Morgan. Bust his ribs in."

Cole groaned and drove a foot at Morgan's shin. Pain laced up his leg. He caught Cole's foot and dragged him out of Gardner's office, the crowd breaking to let him through. He went on, Cole cursing and twisting and trying to jerk free.

His head rapped on a desk, and he cried out in pain again. Morgan took him on through the gate in the railing and out through the front door. He let the foot go then, and pulling Cole to his feet, swung him to the edge of the walk and cracked him on the jaw.

Cole sprawled into the street dust. He sat up, sleeving dirt and sweat from his bruised face. He said thickly: "All right, Morgan. I'm licked, but you never made a bigger mistake in your life."

"Get out of town," Morgan said.

Cole came to his feet, lurching like a drunk, and reached a horse racked in front of the Elite. He tried to get into the saddle and failed. He stood there a moment, trembling, hanging to the horn, knees weak, oblivious to the curious crowd that watched him. He tried again, and this time succeeded in getting a leg across the leather. Reining around the saloon, he took the north road out of town, slumped forward, reeling uncertainly with each jolting step of the horse.

"Who was he?" Dalton asked.

"A gent who thought he was tough," Morgan answered.

Dalton laughed. "Never seen a man take a worse beating. I'd sure hate to be on the other side from you."

"We're on the same side, Clay." Morgan wiped a hand across his face, a sickness crawling through him. There had been no satisfaction in beating Ed Cole. He pushed through the crowd and tramped back to his office. Gardner came in, eyes worried.

"That wasn't good," Gardner said. "Cole won't forget it. You'd better stay in town."

"I'm soft," Morgan muttered. "I should have killed him."

Gardner nodded sober agreement. "Before this is over, you will, or he'll kill you."

# Chapter 18: The Wheel Is Turned

OVERNIGHT THE TEMPERAMENT OF THE CAMP changed. The day Morgan had his fight with Cole the settlers were optimistic and good-humored. The next morning they stood in thick knots along the street, scowling, a sullen anger upon them.

Gardner, taught by long experience to react instantly to a crowd's mood, felt the change and started looking for Morgan. He found him finishing breakfast in the hotel dining room.

"Hell's loose," Gardner said worriedly. "The settlers are standing around with their lower lips hanging down so far they'll trip on them the first step they take."

"First time I've seen you worried," Morgan said, reaching for tobacco and paper.

"First time I have been. You don't reckon they'd listen to Cole?"

"He's not their kind, but they would listen to Royce and Blazer. We'd better get the drawing started."

"We can't. We advertised September 1 and that's what it's got to be."

"What's biting 'em?"

"I don't know. Looks like they'd come in if they had a kick."

223

Morgan sealed his cigarette and slid it into his mouth. "Let's go talk to 'em."

"We can't risk it. That bunch could turn into a mob in a minute. We've got to find somebody we know to tell us what's wrong."

"Let's get hold of Dalton."

They left the hotel, the crowd on the boardwalk making a path for them. Morgan spoke to some he knew. They nodded, faces sullen and resentful, the pressure of their hostility pushing at Morgan and Gardner.

"You're sure right about these boys," Morgan muttered. "Wouldn't take much to turn 'em into a pack of wolves."

They found Dalton at the bar with his Nebraska friends. They faced Morgan and Gardner, Dalton's face showing his resentment. He said darkly, "You played hell, Morgan. Didn't think you was that shortsighted."

"All right, Clay," Morgan said mildly. "Let's have it."

"I had it for supper," Dalton growled. "I don't want no more of it."

"Damn it," Gardner cried in a frenzy. "What are you talking about?"

Dalton snorted and reached for a bottle. "Don't give me that pap. I figgered you was a straight-shooting outfit. Now I'm giving you some advice. You run a straight draw or you'll get a neck-stretching."

Gardner looked at Morgan helplessly. Morgan's cigarette had gone cold in his mouth. His searching mind could find no clue in Dalton's words. He said patiently, "It'll be an honest draw, Clay, but there's something we don't understand. What was it you had for supper?"

Dalton gave him a look rich with scorn. "Hogs, you fool. We took one of them critters and cooked some of it. We couldn't eat it. Nobody else could, neither. The meals in the tent restaurant wasn't no better."

Morgan looked blankly at Gardner, "What hogs?"

"I told you about them," Gardner said defensively. "I contracted with the Sneed boys to butcher some wild hogs. I saw one of the loads they brought in yesterday. The meat looked all right."

"Sure, looked all right," Dalton snorted. "You try eating any?"

"No, but I tell you the meat looked all right."

"I said, 'Did you eat a hunk of it?' " Dalton bellowed. "Tasted like you'd fed them hogs onions."

"Royce said they ate wild hogs all the time . . ."

"So Royce gave you the idea," Morgan said thoughtfully. "I don't know much about the Sneed boys, but they're north rimmers, too."

"I know what Royce is," Gardner began, "but it seemed like a good—"

225

"Clay, I don't know just what's wrong," Morgan broke in, "but I'll find out. There's several hombres around here who don't want the land sale to come off. This hog business is part of the deal."

Doubt struggled through Dalton. "I'd like to believe you, Morgan, but these fellers who came around last night talked mighty straight. They said we was suckers to come out here. Claimed you would crook us on the draw. Good land would go to the Clancys. It was part of a deal you'd made with 'em last spring. They said you was pushing them hogs off on us, 'cause it was the cheapest meat you could get."

It made sense now. Fresh meat that nobody could eat after enjoying the anticipation of it. Then some of the valley settlers showing up and fanning a smoldering fire into a blaze. Morgan asked, "Who were these men?"

"Didn't catch their names, but they live in the valley."

"What'd they look like?"

"One was big. Kind of pig eyes. Other one was smaller. Flat nose. Blue eyes set plumb close together."

"Royce and Blazer," Gardner cried.

"Those are two of the valley men who want us to fail," Morgan said.

"Why?" Dalton asked skeptically.

"Several reasons. One is that they'll be dispossessed as soon as somebody draws their location. You boys are playing their game when you believe 'em. Now, I'm gonna lay my cards on the table. I need your help. We've bought some Clancy beef, but they haven't got the herd down from the hills yet. I'll go see Clancy today, but we haven't got anybody to do the butchering."

"We'll do it for you," Dalton said.

"Then that's fine. Pass the word along what I'm doing. And Gardner, ride out to the lake and see what is wrong with that pork."

Grumbling, Gardner followed Morgan outside. "Clancy will kill you if you go up there."

"I'll take Purdy. Git now. Split the breeze."

Still grumbling, Gardner turned toward the livery stable. Morgan angled across the street to Purdy's office, feeling hostile eyes upon him. There was no overt act. Just sullen silence, like the moments of sticky stillness before the heavens empty upon an earth sucked dry by a torrid sun. Morgan had seen mobs form; he knew the signs, and he didn't like what he saw this morning.

Purdy was pacing the floor of his office, fingers working restlessly through his short hair. He waved a hand toward the street and said, without greeting, "What's the matter with those madmen?" When Morgan told him about the pork, he smiled thinly. "Nobody can eat a hog that's been feeding on tule bulbs. It's like Dalton

227

said. They taste like they'd been eating onions."

"But Gardner said the meat looked good, and the Sneeds claimed they butchered wild hogs every year."

"Sure the meat does look good, but the nesters drive a batch of hogs home and fatten them on grain before they butcher. Besides, I'd say the Sneeds were on Cole's side."

It was done. Nothing that Morgan or Gardner could do would change the settlers' temper except to get Turkey Track beef in today and start Dalton and his friends butchering. It was touch and go, a question whether even good meat could satisfy the contract holders.

Morgan looked around Purdy's office. It seemed no different than it had the first day Morgan was here, but it was different, and the difference lay in Abel Purdy himself. Doc Velie had been wrong about the man and Morgan had been right. A miracle had been performed. Morgan's confidence had restored the heart to this shell of what had once been a courageous man.

"Gardner contracted with Broad Clancy for some beef," Morgan said. "I'm riding out there today."

This was Abel Purdy's test. Rodding a brawling boom town was one thing; facing Broad Clancy was something else, for Clancy had owned Purdy the same as he had owned the storekeeper and the barber and the stableman and the rest. Like Purdy, they could have said they wanted security and that security lasted only as long as Broad Clancy did. But the metamorphosis was complete. Purdy glanced at his star and slowly brought his eyes to Morgan.

"I'll go along for the ride, Murdo. If you have any relatives who want to hear from you, you'd better take time to write to them."

"I don't," Morgan said. "Let's ride."

They left the town fifteen minutes later, skirting the white city of tents and covered wagons, ignoring the sullen stares that followed them out of town. Black clouds were rearing threatening heads along the southwestern sky and a damp wind was breaking through the gap between the Sunsets and Clancy Mountain.

"We're in for a change of weather," Purdy said.

"A storm would play hell with those hombres," Morgan grumbled, "tempers screwed up like they are now."

Purdy turned pale eyes on Morgan. "The world is a more complex thing than most of us realize who live in an island of isolation. Remember my saying that time is a great sea washing around us?" When Morgan nodded, he went on: "I said we'd see how well Broad had built his walls. Now we know. They weren't high enough. I knew it the minute you walked into my office after Flint had shot you. We'd been thinking you were dead. When I saw you, I knew you were immortal."

"My hide ain't that tough," Morgan said.

"You may die this morning, of course. What I meant is that men like you believe in something strongly enough to fight for it, regardless of the vested interests who bring change about and batter down the walls that the Broad Clancys build. This is the same fight that has gone on since the beginning of time, just a skirmish, but the same fight, and we'll always have it."

"Doc Velie said you thought too much."

Purdy smiled meagerly. "Perhaps. Funny thing. I've wanted to be the kind of man Doc Velie is. He was the only one in the valley before you came who wasn't afraid of Clancy. When I heard what you and Doc and Jewell had done, I knew Broad was licked and I was going to help. Security wasn't important. The right to get up and howl when I wanted to was."

"You shoot damned straight for a gent who wears glasses."

Purdy flushed with the praise. "I see all right." He squinted at the spreading gloom of the clouds. "Let's set a faster pace, Murdo."

They held their direction south across the slowly lifting sage flat. Then they were among the buttes, the junipers bigger and more thickly spaced than in the valley. Morgan, staring thoughtfully at the sharp point of Clancy Mountain, wondered if old Broad intended to keep his word.

They circled a butte and, breaking over a ridge, looked down upon a large Turkey Track herd. The cattle were being held in a pocket carpeted by bunchgrass, a creek cutting through the center. Rimrock around three sides made a natural corral so that only a few riders were necessary to hold them. All but two were idling around a fire directly below Morgan.

"Hell, we won't need that many," Morgan mused. "Wonder why he fetched that big a herd?"

"I'm wondering why he brought any," Purdy said.

"He's down there," Morgan pointed to a rider angling toward the fire from the grazing cattle. "We'll ask him."

They dropped down the slope, causing a stirring among the buckaroos when they were seen. One called to Broad Clancy, who looked up, saw Morgan and Purdy, and brought his horse to a gallop. By the time Morgan gained the flat, Clancy had reached the others and dismounted. As he rode up to the fire, Morgan had a feeling that this was what Clancy had expected and planned.

"Howdy," Morgan said civilly, as he reined up.

Clancy did not return the greeting. He stood between the fire and Morgan, spindly legs spread wide. Short John and the rest of the crew were behind him and on the opposite side of the fire. He did not ask Morgan and Purdy to step down. He stood in cold silence, a bitter man, eyes like smoldering emeralds under bushy brows.

There were five men behind Broad Clancy, Short John on the end. Good men for their job, salty, loyal, and ready to fight, but Morgan didn't think it would come to that. A deeper game was being played, and Morgan could guess the reason. Like Ed Cole, old Broad didn't want murder laid to his door if trouble brought an outside lawman to the valley. It meant, then, that Broad had a better idea for smashing the land sale.

"Broad," Purdy said sharply, "if you're planning on burning powder, you'd better get both of us, because I'll take you in for murder if you kill Morgan."

Clancy didn't laugh, as he would have two months before. He had forgotten how to laugh, and Morgan, staring at him, realized only then how much Rip's death had changed him.

"Why didn't you fetch the cows Gardner bought?" Morgan asked.

Still Clancy said nothing. His green eyes stabbed Morgan, probing for something he didn't know. He seemed older and frailer than when Morgan had seen him in the Silver Spur that first day he was in the valley, so frail that it looked as if his bowlegs would crumple under the weight of the heavy gun on his hip.

Clancy asked suddenly, "Did you kill Rip, Morgan?"

"No." Morgan understood it now. Clancy hadn't been sure. Perhaps that was the reason he had called off the hunt when Morgan was wounded. "Tom Carrick did."

"That was what Jewell said," Clancy muttered. "I never knew her to lie, and I don't reckon Josh Morgan's son would lie."

"We want some beef," Purdy cut in.

"Shut up, you damned double-crossing weasel." Clancy was suddenly angry, terribly angry as his stare cut Purdy. He brought his gaze again to Morgan. "What'll happen if you don't get any beef?"

"I'll have trouble," Morgan said frankly, "but you promised Gardner."

"Yeah," Clancy breathed, "and I'll keep my word. I'll have 'em within a mile of town tomorrow night."

"The boys are on the prod. I've got to have some today."

"They've got to rest up," Clancy said. "Good grass here."

"Then have your boys cut out twenty head and me and Purdy'll haze 'em to town. You can bring the rest tomorrow."

Clancy rubbed his narrow chin, as if weighing a decision. The men behind him relaxed. Even Short John, who had always looked scared whenever Morgan had seen him, now appeared relieved.

"All right," Clancy said finally. "Slim. Rory. Cut out twenty head. Push 'em down the creek." Then, for no understandable reason except that he had held it back so long, fury gripped the little cowman. It painted his face purple, brought his gnarled fist up to threaten Morgan. "Damn the woman who gave you birth, Morgan. If I thought you'd killed Rip, I'd gun you down, but I'm letting you live because I want to see your clodbusters put a rope around your neck. Now get to hell out of here."

"We don't need that many cows," Morgan said.

"You'll get 'em whether you need 'em or not," Clancy screamed, "and you'll eat your beef in hell. I said to vamoose. Git, afore I plug you."

Morgan and Purdy swung their horses down the creek, Purdy asking, "How do you figure it, Murdo?"

"I couldn't figger out in the first place why he promised to let us have the beef and I can't now." Morgan twisted a smoke, frowning at it. "And I can't figger out how he's going to get the settlers to hang us, but he was confident, Abel. Mighty confident."

# Chapter 19: Search

IT WAS DARK BY THE TIME MORGAN STABLED his black and found an empty table in the hotel dining room. Jewell, seeing him come in, called someone to the desk and sat down at Morgan's table. She said, "It's been a mean day."

"What happened?"

"Nothing. There was some wild talk, but Jim Carrick got Mossbrain to drive his water wagon and he stayed in town. He talked some sense into most of them."

"I owe a lot to Jim," he said soberly. "I owe a lot to several people, come to think of it."

"No one ever did anything worth while alone, Murdo." She rose and went back to the kitchen for coffee. When she returned with two cups, she asked, "Have you seen Peg?"

"No."

The waitress came for his order, and he was glad of the interruption. He did not want to discuss Peg with Jewell. After the waitress left, he said, "I saw Broad."

She showed surprise. "Was there trouble?"

"No." He told her what had happened. "Doesn't make sense. I've been trying to add it up ever since Gardner told me about the deal, but I don't get any answers."

"He's a careful man," Jewell said, troubled. "He has a trick that he's sure will work, or he wouldn't have let it go this long."

"Maybe he's waiting for Cole to do the job."

"Maybe, but if Cole doesn't get it done, Dad will still have his trick. Then if the law moves in, he'll be in the clear." She rose, and stood looking at him, her full-lipped mouth sweetly set. "Be careful," she said, and left the dining room.

Morgan cruised the street after he had eaten; the campfires were like pointed red stars flickering across the flat. Lightning ate at the edge of the sky, and thunder rolled across the empty miles. Sage smell, sharpened by distant rain, was carried to him by the night wind. It was a dark world, the rimrock entirely lost to sight, the lights of Irish Bend and the sprawling camp a bright core in an otherwise black valley.

The street was deserted, the saloons nearly so. The settlers were gathered in their tents or around their campfires, the topic of their conversation likely being Murdo Morgan. He paused in front of his dark office, smoking a cigarette and thinking about these people who had crossed half a continent to follow a dream. He wanted to talk to some of them to feel out their sentiment, but his appearance in camp might start trouble. On the other hand he could not afford to let them think he had been bluffed into inactivity. Making up his mind that way, he tossed his cigarette stub into the dust, slanted across the street, went around the Silver Spur and on into the sage flat to the camp.

The butchering was still going on and there was a moving column of settlers coming empty-handed and leaving with as much meat as they needed for their party. Jim Carrick was helping, and when he saw Morgan in the fringe of firelight, he called out in his robust voice, "Clancy beef ain't so bad, Murdo, when the right folks eat it."

"Better'n pork, maybe," Morgan said.

Dalton wiped a bloody hand across his pants. "That's the truest thing you ever said, mister. The boys have got a little different idea of you than they had."

"Royce or Blazer around?"

"They was a while ago, but I ain't seen 'em for quite a spell."

Morgan thought of searching for them and decided against it. These people would not understand if he found them and killed them. He stood in silence, watching men come and go, thinking how much difference a full belly meant. It was not a case of starving; it was a matter of a promise being kept. In that keeping he had stripped the solid ground away from Royce and Blazer.

He returned to town and climbed the stairs to

his hotel room. He undressed and smoked a last cigarette, thinking of his father, lucky in love, but without the strength and toughness to bring his dreams to fruition.

It rained during the night. Daylight came slowly, fighting through the dark overcast. Morgan had an early breakfast, and before he had finished eating, Gardner joined him.

"What happened yesterday?" Morgan asked.

"The Sneeds were getting ready to butcher another batch of hogs," Gardner answered. "They said they knew the meat wasn't any good, but I didn't ask them, so they didn't figure it was their business to tell me."

"Then there ain't no doubt about them being with Cole," Morgan said.

Gardner nodded somberly. "I paid them off. They were damned hostile, saying we didn't keep our bargain."

Morgan rose. "Stay in town today."

"What are you going to do?"

"I'm taking a ride. Cole's around somewhere. I'm done waiting."

"You've got to be here tomorrow."

"Why? The drawing ain't till Monday."

"I'm calling a meeting of the contract holders in the morning to elect three trustees. I talked to Dalton about it yesterday. The way things have been going, I thought we'd better have them on the platform during the drawing."

"I'll be here," Morgan said.

He was back late that night, bone-weary and disappointed. He had found no trace of Cole or his men. The north-rim settlers shook their heads and said in grim honesty they had not seen anything of Blazer or Royce for more than a week.

The election went off Saturday morning with less friction than might have been expected. Dalton, Jale Miller from Iowa, and a somber-faced Missourian named Hugh Frawley were the winners. Morgan had no fault to find with Dalton, but Frawley and Miller had listened to Royce and Blazer.

After the election Gardner explained the procedure that would be followed through the entire drawing. The settlers listened in silence, and when he was done, filed out of the big tent without even a murmur of talk rising from them. It was not, Morgan knew, a healthy silence.

Clancy had brought his herd in as he had agreed and was holding them south of the camp. Dalton had butchered Friday night and would again Saturday night.

"The beef stalled things off," Dalton told Morgan after the election, "but it didn't make everybody forget what Royce and Blazer have been saying. The boys figger they'll wait and see what happens when the drawing starts. There are some things about Gardner's scheme they don't like."

Again Morgan searched for Cole, making a

wide swing across the west end of the valley, a nagging sense of urgency riding with him. If he didn't find Cole, the man would be with Royce and Blazer at the drawing, free to work the crowd into a howling mob.

But luck was not with Morgan. He returned to Irish Bend, hours after dark, the afternoon wasted. There were a thousand places to hide, and Morgan could not search all of them. He had known that, but he had hoped to flush Cole out of his hiding place by showing himself. It was a long chance, offering himself as bait and giving Cole the odds, but it was a better gamble than waiting until the drawing.

"Don't try it again," Jewell said at breakfast. "Don't push your luck too hard."

"I make my luck," he said roughly.

"You don't really mean that, Murdo. Some of your luck is beyond your power to make. Call it Providence if you want to."

He ate in silence, thinking about what she had said. There were times when he didn't understand her, when she seemed like Abel Purdy, hating what had been done but lacking the strength to change Broad Clancy's ways. Yet there was one important difference between her and Purdy. He had chosen the valley, taking with it the things he hated; life had placed Jewell here. Purdy's battle had been with himself; Jewell had made a stand against her father, and that had taken the kind of courage Morgan had never found before in a woman.

"What are you thinking about?" she asked suddenly.

"You," he said, "and what's ahead."

She rose, her face utterly sober, and he knew they were thinking of the same thing, of Broad Clancy, who was with his herd a mile from town, waiting to make a final move that Morgan could not foresee, a move that Clancy was certain would doom the drawing to failure and break Morgan.

"The settlers are having a service in the big tent this morning," Jewell said. "Will you go with me?"

It had been a long time since he had gone to church. He hesitated, considering his motives for going and wondering what the settlers would think if they saw him there.

"Please come," she urged. "We've never had a church here. I've always wanted one, but if a preacher did drift into the valley, Dad would send him on."

"I'll go," he said.

Morgan shaved and put on a clean shirt. He considered his gun for a moment and decided to leave it. When he met Jewell in the lobby, he saw her eyes drop to his hip. She brought her gaze to his face, a quick smile sweetening the corners of her mouth.

"I was afraid you'd wear it," she said.

A piano had been brought from the Silver Spur and placed on the platform. Mrs. Clay Dalton played and Jim Carrick led the hymns in his booming voice. Hugh Frawley, the Missourian who had been elected trustee, preached.

"This is to be our home," Frawley said after he had finished his sermon. "It's fitting and right that on this first Sunday after we have reached the valley we should have a service that'll please the Lord. We've got land to clear and houses to build. We'll have a school. If the devil ain't too strong, we'll have a church. There's some who are not here to worship with us. There's drinking and gambling going on this minute, and them that don't love the Lord are a-plotting and a-scheming to bust what we're trying to do. This is our chance to own our homes. We ain't gonna let nobody crook us out of it."

Frawley's eyes were pinned on Morgan. "The devil's always been smart at fixing himself up. Appearances may deceive us mortals, but the Lord He ain't fooled by the way a man looks. It's what's in his heart that the Lord looks at."

Later, after Frawley had prayed a long prayer asking for the Lord's blessing on this new land and those who had come here to find homes, Morgan walked out of the tent, Jewell beside him. Buck Carrick had been there with Peg. She

242

hurried him away, not looking at Morgan, but Buck kept turning back, a triumphant grin on his face. Morgan, nodding at him, wondered what Jim would say.

"You'll have dinner with me, won't you?" Jewell asked when they reached the hotel. "We're having chicken. I asked Gardner." She paused and added hesitantly, "And the Frawleys."

"I never turn down chicken," Morgan said.

They ate upstairs in the hotel parlor, a strange, too-silent meal. Hugh Frawley's suspicions were a disturbing factor in the little room. Then, over the second cup of coffee, Jewell said: "Mr. Frawley, Murdo and I know why you said what you did this morning, but you're wrong. There are so many things you don't understand."

"I know what the devil does to a man who has money." Frawley waggled a finger at Gardner. "You've made a fortune selling land and I've had to work for every penny I've got, work and sweat and break my back."

"I had a fortune when I started selling land," Gardner said angrily. "I've kept about even in the game and I won't do any better here. I'm putting in a reservoir and a ditch system. Who'll do it if I don't, and what do you reckon it'll cost me?"

"I don't know," Frawley admitted, "but I've heard some of the old settlers talk. I know how this land grant was stolen in the first place."

"All right," Morgan said testily. "It was a steal,

243

but I'm doing something about it. If I hadn't gambled everything I had, you wouldn't be here. If the drawing fails, it'll be on account of men like you who don't trust Gardner and me."

"A man can't fool the Lord by coming to church," Frawley began piously. "I can't look into your heart—"

"Mr. Frawley," Jewell broke in, "Murdo went to church this morning because I asked him to. I believe any community is better because it has a church. You're about to convince me I'm wrong."

"I don't want to do that," Frawley said, as if deeply hurt.

A knock at the door brought Jewell to her feet. She said, "Excuse me," and stepping around Morgan's chair, opened the door.

One of the Sneed brothers stood in the hall, a dark thin man with vacant eyes that seemed to be continually looking for something he could not find. He mumbled, "Morgan here?"

Morgan rose and came to the door. "What is it, Sneed?"

"It ain't nothing." Sneed's low forehead wrinkled in surprise. "I rode plumb into town to do you a favor. Heerd you wanted somebody."

"Who?"

"Ed Cole."

"Where is he?"

"At Royce's place. Cole, he sent me to tell you

he reckoned you was a-scairt to come after him. Alone."

"Tell him I'll be there."

Sneed wiped tobacco drool from the corners of his mouth. "Sure, I'll tell him. Then I'm gonna git to hell out of there and watch. Oughtta be a fair-to-middling fight." Turning, he lumbered down the stairs.

Jewell caught Morgan's arm. "Don't go, Murdo. Don't you see what it is?"

"I see, all right. Cole set up a trap that he figgers will bring me on the run. He's right. It will."

"Take Purdy," Gardner said.

"It's my job," Morgan said quietly. "If I took anybody else, it'd scare Cole off, and I've got to get him before he boogers up the drawing tomorrow."

Jewell waited until he came back from his room, shell belt buckled around him, gun in his holster. He winked at her. "Mighty good chicken. Didn't think there was a hen in the valley."

"You just have to know where to look," she said with forced levity. Then she touched his arm, her face showing the force of her emotions, her eyes on his high-boned face. "Be careful, Murdo."

Jewell watched his tall wide back until he crossed the lobby and was out of sight. She turned to Frawley then, her voice weighted by contempt, "How can you hate and suspect a man who has done so much for you?"

Frawley's thin-lipped mouth opened in surprise. "What's he done for me except to make a deal with your father so he'll get the best land, while me and my neighbors came out here in good faith."

"You're a fool to believe the lies of Blazer and Royce," she flung at him. "I suppose it's because you don't understand. You came from a settled community where people had respect for law. We don't have it here. It's something that has to be built. Can you do it by preaching sermons?"

Hugh Frawley rubbed a lean jaw, his face thoughtful. "No, I can't."

"It takes men like Murdo Morgan to make law mean something. Some men never learn except at the point of a gun. Blazer and Royce are that way. You didn't see them in church, did you?"

But Frawley was not convinced. "We'll see how honest your friend Morgan is. Tomorrow."

# Chapter 20: The Trap

THE CLOUDS HAD BROKEN WHEN MORGAN left town so that the sky was a shifting checkerboard of blue and white. The sun, working into the clear, threw a brief heat upon Morgan's back and then withdrew it when the clouds swept in and dark shadow filtered across the sage flat again.

Topping the ridge that lay west of the lake, Morgan rode down to the tule swamp that stretched for miles along the edge. Royce's cabin squatted ahead of him, Peg's well kept lawn an emerald island between the empty desert and the dismal gray water of the lake. Royce had been too busy conspiring with Cole to do any farming. His hay had not been cut; last year's stack stood untouched.

There was no eagerness in Murdo Morgan. He was close now to the completion of a job he had been trying to do for days. The time was past when he thrilled to the buck of a gun in his hand, the conflict and the clash, the test of gunspeed. Maturity had brought judgment and a depth of purpose. This was just another dirty job that had to be done. He felt no bitterness for Ed Cole. That had gone from him when he had beaten the man in Gardner's office.

The only thing that worried Morgan was Peg's presence in the cabin. Now, eyes fixed on Royce's buildings, he thought with sudden relief that it would be finished in the open. Four men were loitering between the corral and the house. Then, as if seeing Morgan for the first time, they stepped into saddles and turned their horses toward him.

Morgan drew his gun, wondering about this. It was not like Ed Cole to fight in the open. The men were still too far away to be identified. Perhaps Cole had stayed in the cabin and had offered a price high enough to induce his men to go after Morgan.

A hog crashed through the tules. Startled, Morgan whipped around in the saddle, eyes swinging involuntarily toward the lake. Only then did he realize how tense he had become, how the steady pressure that danger had laid upon him had tightened his nerves. He brought his gaze back to the four men bearing down upon him. It was wrong. All wrong. Cole was on one end, Royce next, the Sneeds on the other end. *Arch Blazer was not in the party!*

Instinctively, Morgan pulled up his horse. Blazer should be with Cole. Then it happened. No warning of any kind. He heard the loop swish around him, felt it tighten. There was one brief moment of realization that disaster had closed in upon him, a wild clawing hope that he could get the man behind him before the four in front closed in. The hope died the instant it was born. His arms were pinioned at his sides. He was jerked out of the saddle. He hit the ground, a hard jolting fall, and threshed in the tules, struggling to gain his feet and get his arms free.

He glimpsed Blazer's face, wicked in triumph, glimpsed the blur of the down-sweeping gun barrel. Pain exploded in his head. He twisted and fired, a wild shot that missed by three feet. Blazer hit him again, and strength went out of Morgan's knees and he fell into the muck and darkness washed in around him.

Blazer removed his rope, picked up Morgan's gun, and waded through the shallow water to dry ground. When Cole and the others rode up, he swung a meaty hand toward the unconscious Morgan. "Want me to give him a slug?"

"No, you fool," Cole said angrily. "Put his gun back."

"Why, hell . . ."

"Put his gun back," Cole cried, rage gripping him. "We're making dust. Purdy and Gardner'll be out here and we want this to look like an accident. His horse threw him, he got knocked cold, and a wild hog ate him. They can't hang us for that."

Grumbling, Blazer slid the gun back into Morgan's holster, drove a boot toe into his ribs and stomping back, climbed up behind Royce. He said bitterly, "That hombre takes a lot of killing, Ed."

"He'll get plenty lying there." Whistling softly, Cole touched up his horse and swung around the tules, his men following him.

Morgan lay motionless for a long time, the sun beating down upon him. When he regained consciousness, one side of his face was in the mud. Lifting his head, he clawed the muck away, and crawled to solid ground, a warning thought filtering through his numbed brain. There were five men out there who would blow his head off the minute he showed it.

Slowly the tide of memory washed back through him. He'd had his gun in his hand when he'd been yanked out of his saddle. Instinctively, a hand dropped to holster. The gun was there. Reaching the hard-crusted ground, he lay belly flat, puzzling over this. They'd had their chance and he'd been helpless. That's the way Ed Cole would have wanted it. He held up his hat, but there was no sound of guns. He came slowly to his feet, swaying until the dizziness passed. No one was in sight.

Morgan studied the tracks. Cole and his crew had ridden on. Turning, he stumbled toward Royce's cabin, trying to understand this and failing. Then he saw Peg ride out of the Royce yard toward him. He stopped and wiped his face with a hand and shook his head. It seemed as if Cole had lost his mind.

Peg's yell came to him, muffled by the distance. He raised his head and looked at her. She was waving wildly to him. Then she pulled her rifle from the boot and put her horse into a run. Morgan's first thought was that Cole's men were hiding and now were lining their sights on him. Turning, he stopped dead still, paralyzed by what he saw. If he lived to be a million years old, he would never see a more terrifying sight in either reality or a nightmare.

A wild boar was charging him, foaming at the mouth, his great tusks terrible weapons capable of ripping a man into bloody shreds. In that one horrible moment the hog looked as long as a fence rail and four or five feet high, a spindly-rumped, long-snouted monster that would not be stopped short of death. His bristles along his backbone were up, his tail lifted, ears forward, eyes filled with diabolical madness.

Morgan's first impulse was to run. He started away from the lake toward the high sage-covered ground and knew at once he had no chance of outrunning the hog on foot. The thought flashed through his mind that this must be a nightmare. It was too fantastic to be real.

He took three long strides and wheeled back. This was no nightmare. It was a trap spawned in the fetid depths of Cole's cunning brain, a trap that, unless luck was with Murdo Morgan, would bring death to him without the slightest suspicion pointing to Cole or Royce or the others.

Morgan held his ground then and drew his gun. Panic was in him. He had listened to campfire tales of men caught on foot and ripped to pieces by the razor-sharp tusks of such a beast. If he could have had his choice, he would have fought a grizzly or a longhorn bull and considered his chances better.

He eared back the hammer of his .45. He found himself trembling as he tried to line his sights on the boar. If Cole had wanted to disarm him, he'd have unloaded the gun. *Morgan hadn't looked.* This was something that had never entered his mind. He had simply dropped his hand to holster and found the gun. Now his life and the success of the drawing depended on the five bullets in his Colt . . . if there were bullets there.

Now, as so often when a man's life hangs by the finest thread, thoughts flashed through his mind, of his father and his father's dream, of Broad Clancy, who would not, even in his extremity, have used a trap like this; of Cole, whom he had once thought of as his friend, and of Jewell Clancy.

Taking his time, he squeezed trigger. The sound of the shot was thunder loud, a welcome sound to Morgan. Cole had not unloaded the gun. It was a clean miss. Dirt lifted far behind the hog. He had held too high.

The boar didn't pause or turn. He came on, directly at Morgan, his pig brain focused on one evil design. He was close now, driven by a senseless hate. No nightmare could have conjured up a slobbering creature like this, given him such fury-filled eyes, and equipped him with destructive weapons like his tusks.

Again Morgan fired. Panic was gone from him now. Here was an enemy, more horrible than any other he had met, but still an enemy, and must be dealt with accordingly. The slug struck the boar in the snout and brought him to a pause, but only for an instant. He rushed on, drooling blood and slobber, impelled by some strange long-dormant instinct that could not be denied, a heritage, perhaps, coming down through aeons of time and countless generations of hogs extending back through the ages to the distant day when all animals were enemies of man, and man was the enemy of every four-legged or crawling thing.

This man had a thunder stick that spat fire and smoke. It stung, but the hairy man with a silent stringed weapon could shoot feathered shafts that stung, too. This man, like the hairy one, could be ripped open and destroyed, could be brought down from the lofty position to which his long hind legs had lifted him.

It was the same old struggle between man and

his enemy, shifted from some fern-grown swamp to the tule-lined shore of Paradise Lake, from some forgotten day before recorded history to this day when civilized men came to grips over a sparsely settled valley. But there had been no Cole in the fern-grown swamp.

Morgan shot and spun aside as the hog charged past. The bullet raked the boar's shoulder, a wasted bullet, for the wound was of no more importance than the scratch of a splintered juniper limb. The boar came at Morgan again. This time the bullet found its mark, tearing through one tiny wicked eye. The boar dropped at Morgan's feet. He was still in his death throes, working the dirt into bloody mud when Peg reined up.

"I tried to get here sooner," Peg said hoarsely. "I knew what they were going to do. Cole's afraid of a murder charge, but he wanted you out of the way before the drawing."

Morgan wiped sweat from his face, trembling now that it was over. There was one bullet left in his gun. He said bitterly, "They figgered they'd knock me cold and one of them critters would finish me."

"That's right. Purdy would call it an accident. Cole said that if you weren't at the drawing, it would be easier to get the crowd worked into a mob. They'd upset everything and put the land sale back so far it wouldn't get going until it was too late to pay the bank. Then Cole would take over."

Morgan stared at the dead boar. He turned away, a sick emptiness in his stomach. "I've seen some wicked-looking critters, but that's the worst I ever saw when I was awake and sober. He'd weigh six, maybe seven hundred pounds if he was fat."

"The settlers look out for them when they go after the young hogs," Peg said. "All of them say they'd rather meet up with a grizzly."

Turning back, Morgan touched the boar's head with a boot toe. "Look at those tusks. Four inches long or more."

"It would take Cole to think of it. I was crazy enough to let them know I heard what they were up to, so they tied me on the bed. I couldn't get loose any sooner."

"They made a mistake when they left me my gun."

"Royce argued with him over that. Cole had to have everything just right. Wouldn't even let them take the shells out. He says he's the one who will sell the land after the bank takes the grant, and he can't afford to have his reputation questioned. Cole thought a boar would find you sooner than this one did."

"If Cole knew that you . . ."

"He would have come back and shut my mouth for good," she said bitterly. "Royce isn't my father. I found that out this morning. My folks were killed by the Piutes. I suppose I should thank him for raising me, but I don't."

"I thought I'd finish it today," Morgan said heavily as he loaded his gun.

Her eyes searched his face as if seeking the answer to a question that had long been in her mind. "Get up behind me. Your horse is in the yard. I want to go back to the cabin for a few things anyhow. I can't stay here now."

"No," he agreed. "You've stayed too long."

They rode in silence, Morgan nursing a dull regret. He had made a long-odds bet in springing Cole's trap, gambling his life on the chance that he would have an opportunity to kill Cole. Then, and then only could he be sure of a peaceful drawing in the morning. He had failed, and tomorrow would bring its violence.

Peg reined up in front of the cabin. Morgan dismounted and helped her down. She stood close to him for a moment, hungry eyes again searching his face. She turned into the house and went on into her bedroom. Morgan stayed in the front room and smoked a cigarette. There was evidence of a fight in the upended chairs and litter on the floor. He had never seen the place in disorder before. Minutes later, when Peg came out of her bedroom, he asked about it.

"I took Cole's money last spring," she said frankly. "He thought I'd sell you out. That was why I took it. As long as they thought I was on their side, they talked in front of me. Today, when they started their scheming, I lost my head and told Cole what he was." She motioned around the room. "We had a little trouble before they got me tied."

He saw, now that the scarf was off her head, that her hair was in disarray and that there was a dark bruise high on her left cheek. He said: "Thanks for the help you've given me. If I didn't have friends in the valley, I'd have been dead a long time ago."

"I wanted to save your life," she said tonelessly, "but you didn't need my help today the way you needed Jewell Clancy's when you were wounded."

"You saved my life the day Rip was here."

Pleased, she said, "That seems a long time ago." She turned into her bedroom. "I want to fix my hair. Come on in, Murdo."

He followed her to the door and pausing there, put a shoulder against the jamb. He rolled a smoke, thinking how well she had furnished her room with the little she had had, and admiring the neatness and color of it. He smoked in silence, the desire to talk gone from him. He stood, slack-muscled and passive, feeling the letdown that comes after a close escape from death.

When she was done, black hair combed sleekly

back and tied with a red ribbon in the way she always wore it, she turned on her bench and smiled.

It was a warm personal smile. He felt suddenly uncomfortable, for he sensed that she would look at no other man in quite the same way she was looking at him now. The knowledge shocked him. This was a different Peg Royce from the girl whose gay laugh he had heard that night at the Smith shack. She had been so certain of herself, of her ability to hold and control men. Now that assurance was gone, and in its place there was a humility that seemed strange in her.

"It's funny, Murdo," she said. "The first time I saw you I knew you were the man, but I had to talk big like I did to Rip and Buck. It didn't work with you."

He held his silence, suddenly embarrassed as he sensed what she was going to say. If he had not come to the valley, she would probably have been married to Buck Carrick by now. Now Buck would never be the same to her.

"Do you have to go on fighting, Murdo?"

"It's what I've done most of my life."

"You could make a deal with Cole or Broad Clancy. You'd have all the money you want. We could ride away together."

He shook his head, angry with her. "There's always the little fellows who need help. That's

258

why I bought the land grant. It's why I came back."

"But they don't think you're helping them. Royce and Blazer were bragging this morning about how the fool settlers believed what they said about you taking their money and cheating them out of the good land in the draw."

"I'll still help them."

She came to him, face lifted to his, red lips lightly pressed. "It just isn't my luck, is it? I love the wrong man. I won't use you to get what I want like I said that time. You will use me. I'll do whatever you ask me to do."

She wanted him to kiss her, but this time she would force it from him. Again, as she always had, her presence set up a turbulence in him, but it was not a free turbulence, as it had been. Jewell Clancy was in his mind and he knew, as he had known before, that she would always be there, no matter what happened between him and her father, no matter what the future held for him and Peg Royce.

Morgan stepped into the other room and dropped his cigarette stub into the stove. He said, "Ready to ride?"

"It's that Clancy woman, isn't it?" Peg cried in a sudden burst of fury. "I've known all the time, I guess. I just wouldn't believe it." He moved toward the door, not answering. "All right, Murdo." Her tone was flat, lifeless. "I'm ready to ride." She picked up a bundle she had tied and followed him out of the room. "Where will I stay in town?"

"I'll ask Jewell to give you a room."

She stopped, shrinking away from him. "Why do you hate me, Murdo?"

He swung back to face her. "I don't hate you, Peg. I'm grateful for what you've done."

"Grateful," she murmured, making no effort to hide the hurt that was in her. "That's something, but it isn't enough. I won't quit trying, Murdo. I'll make you see me. Someday."

An hour later they met Purdy and Gardner and a dozen others. Morgan did not see that Jewell was with them until he reined up.

"A miracle?" Purdy asked.

"Something like that." Morgan told them what had happened. He pinned his eyes on Jewell's face, doubt touching him. "Peg can't stay out here after this. Can you find a room for her?"

Jewell gave Peg a small smile. Peg, her eyes cold, smiled back. It was a challenge given and a challenge answered. Jewell brought her gaze back to Morgan. "I don't have an empty room, Murdo, but there's a double bed in my room. She can sleep with me."

Peg said through tight lips, "Thank you."

"You need a guardian, Murdo," Purdy grumbled. "You sure didn't have any business riding into that. I got a bunch together as soon as

Gardner told me, but I thought I'd be too late."

They swung back to town, but Morgan only half listened to the talk. Peg had looked at him as if he had betrayed her, and he could not understand it.

# Chapter 21: Land Sale

MORGAN WAS SHAVING ON MONDAY MORNING
when Gardner tapped on his door. He called,
"Come in," and Gardner, opening the door,
motioned a stocky man into the room.

"Morgan, meet Post Office Inspector Bartell,"
Gardner said. "He got in on the late stage last
night."

Morgan shook hands and indicated a chair.
"Glad to know you, Bartell. Sit down. I'll be done
in a minute and we'll go down for breakfast."

Gardner paced to the window. "Damned mean
day," he said sourly. "Sticky. We're in for a
thundershower. Weather's as jittery as a pregnant
woman. Tempers ruffle easy on a day like this."

The inspector smiled as he lighted a cigar.
"They'll just have to ruffle. We can't change the
law."

Morgan turned from the mirror. "What law?"

"The government prohibits land allotments by
lottery. That's why I'm here."

"I know that. So do you, Gardner."

Gardner shuffled uneasily. "I didn't tell you,
you having that trouble with Cole like you did,
but yesterday the trustees got hold of me and
demanded that the drawing be made a straight

lottery. No bidding. They claimed that by allowing the bidding we're opening the way for Clancy to buy in his buildings and anything he wants. They don't have much money. Clancy does, so he can outlast them. In other words, they claim they should get each tract for the contract price of $200."

"Hell, it says right on the contract that there'll be opportunity to bid on each tract before it's knocked off," Morgan exploded. "I told you the first time—"

"I know," Gardner said gloomily, "but Frawley and Miller were pretty hostile. Been listening to Royce and Blazer again, I guess. Frawley and Miller said they couldn't guarantee that the men would stay in line if Clancy bid in a few choice tracts."

For a moment there was no sound but the steady scratching of razor on stubble. This was the trick Clancy was depending on, the reason for him holding back. He could not be blamed for what would happen today, and it would not make any trouble for him even if the governor sent a special investigator to the valley.

There was no talk until Morgan finished shaving. Gardner fidgeted by the window; Bartell sat motionless, pulling steadily on his cigar. Morgan put on his shirt, buckled his gun belt around him, and slid into his coat. He said, "Let's have breakfast."

"What are you going to do?" Gardner asked.

"Nothing," Morgan said flatly. "They'll abide by the contract."

After breakfast Morgan waited in the lobby for Jewell and Peg. They came down together, both smiling when he said, "Good morning." He could not tell from their composed faces what had passed between them.

"This is your last warning," he said. "That platform won't be the safest place in town today."

"It'll be a good place to watch from if there's trouble," Peg said.

Morgan looked helplessly at Jewell, who smiled as if this was an ordinary day instead of the biggest one Paradise Valley had ever known. She said, "I wouldn't miss it."

"All right," he said. "We'd better get over there."

They followed the boardwalk to the Stockmen's Bank, angled across the intersection to the store, and moved around it to the big tent. Purdy, waiting outside, motioned to Morgan and stepped back.

"Broad Clancy ain't here but Short John is," Purdy said when Morgan joined him. "He's got six cowhands with him. What do you think he's up to?"

"I'm guessing he'll make a bid on a tract of land," Morgan said. "Then hell will blow up in our faces."

Purdy stared across the sage flat, troubled eyes blinking behind thick lenses. He said, "Cole's in there with the Sneeds, Blazer, and Royce. Pretty close to the front and on the other side of the tent from Short John. I thought of arresting them, but I don't have any real charge and I was afraid of what the settlers would do."

"That's right," Morgan agreed. "I've got a hunch I can stop them. Come on up to the platform."

Purdy nodded and turning back to Peg and Jewell, moved beside Morgan up the middle aisle. Every bench was filled and men were packed around the sides and rear of the tent. There were a thousand settlers here, Morgan guessed, perhaps more. He spoke to some he knew and they spoke back civilly enough. He thought they had, as Dalton had said, decided to wait and see. There was hope in that, but the material for an explosion was still present.

Morgan stepped back when he reached the platform, motioning for Peg and Jewell to go ahead and mentally cursed Gardner for insisting on them being here. It was not going to be the kind of show Gardner had anticipated. Morgan climbed to the platform, Purdy remaining on the ground.

"Eight o'clock," Gardner said.

Morgan nodded, eyes sweeping the platform. The bulk of Gardner's office crew had moved over here. There was a jumble of tables and chairs, books and boxes and record sheets, and Morgan wondered if any kind of order could be kept once the drawing was under way. Gardner had seated Peg and Jewell behind a table at the front of the platform, two boxes in front of them. The trustees were on the other side of the table, the post-office inspector beyond them.

Stepping to the front of the platform, Morgan felt a sudden chill ravel down his spine. Ed Cole's handsome face stood out in the packed mass. He was smiling, a contemptuous smile, as if this was the moment he had long enjoyed in anticipation. It was Morgan's moment, too, but now that it was here, he wished he were a million miles away. His head was a vacuum; no words came to his tongue.

Gardner whispered, "Get it started."

Morgan licked dry lips, eyes turning to Jewell. It seemed to him he could hear her say again, "Do what you have to do, Murdo." He swung back to the ocean of faces, the chill gone from his spine. This had to go. It was too close to the end to miss now. *It had to go.*

"On behalf of the Cascade & Paradise Land Company," Morgan began, "I welcome you and wish you prosperity and happiness in your new homes. Some of the land that will be drawn is good only for grazing and will go out in 1,000-acre blocks. The better land has been cut into smaller tracts ranging from 160 acres down. The 10-acre tracts are all located south of the lake, where irrigation is not necessary. You will find no better land out of doors, and I know you won't find another place in the West where you can get a clear title to a good farm for $20 an acre or less.

"I have no promises to make about a railroad, but history tells us that steel will be laid to any place in the United States where production is big enough to make it worth while. That production depends on you, but one thing I can promise. Grant Gardner will see that you have water." Morgan turned to Gardner. "Want to say something, Grant?"

Gardner rose and stepped up beside Morgan. "When Morgan came to me several months ago, I was frankly pessimistic about his project. When I saw this valley I changed my mind. I promised him I'd build the reservoir and ditch system if the type of settlers who came here looked like men who would work. Well, boys, you do. I'm an old hand at this business. I know I didn't make a mistake in you and you didn't make a mistake in trying this valley. I'll make a promise now. By next spring work will start on the ditches and as many reservoirs as we find necessary."

The clapping was perfunctory. Morgan waited until it died. The feeling was wrong. Suspicion rose from this closely packed crowd of men and pressed against him. Dynamite was here, the fuse attached. Cole's contemptuous smile was a constant thing, his face a magnet drawing Morgan's gaze. Morgan's lips tightened. Jaw muscles bulged. He was too close to the fulfillment of a dream to let it die.

"One more thing before we start the drawing," Morgan went on. "The matter of doing away with the bidding and making this drawing a lottery was brought up by the trustees. We're willing to grant your request, but Uncle Sam ain't."

Morgan motioned toward Bartell. "We have a post-office inspector with us who will remain for the length of the drawing. The minute we take away the right to bid he'll close us down, so I have a request to make. Don't take advantage of the opportunity to bid. Accept your tract of land as it is drawn. We don't want more than the price of your contract. If there is bidding and the prices run over $200, the balance will be divided and refunded to you."

Cole jerked forward, suddenly sober, the scornful smile swept from his lips. A sense of triumph surged through Morgan. He had cut away much of the ground from which Cole had expected to launch his attack.

"The procedure has been explained, so I won't repeat it," Morgan hurried on. "We have two ladies on the platform, Miss Peg Royce and Miss Jewell Clancy, who will make the drawing. Grant Gardner will handle the auctioning. We promised to pay the traveling expenses and give $25 for your living expenses while here to any of you who represent twenty or more contracts. If you've got that coming and haven't collected, visit the cashier in our main office and you'll be paid."

Morgan paused, sensing a change sweep over the crowd. Despite the doubts and suspicion that Royce and Blazer had planted, these men wanted to believe in the inherent fairness of the company. Cole, Morgan saw, sensed that same intangible tide sweep the crowd. He sat hunched forward, gaze fixed on Morgan, his eyes bright and wicked and entirely lacking their usual guile.

Swinging to Gardner, Morgan said, "All right, Grant."

Morgan stepped down from the platform and joined Purdy. The lawman laid a hand on Morgan's shoulder. "I didn't know you were a public speaker, Murdo."

"Hell, I'm not," Morgan said sheepishly. "For a minute there I couldn't have told you my name."

Purdy laughed softly. "I saw you look at Jewell and everything came back. I think you licked Cole on that business of bidding."

"He looks licked," Morgan said and turned his gaze to Gardner.

"You have your clearance receipt, men," Gardner was saying in a crisp businesslike tone. "As soon as your name is called, or if you are

269

acting for an absent contract holder, make your bid for $200. If I knock the tract off to you, come around to the back of the platform, pay the balance you owe the company, and you will be given your papers.

"Yesterday we had a conference with the trustees. They requested that if any errors are found in the titles they should be corrected at company expense and that the company make the deeds to the contract holders instead of the trustees as stated in the contract. The company has accepted those changes."

Gardner moved around Jewell's chair and stood between her and Peg. He said: "In one box we have slips of paper with the number and acreage of each tract. They have been well shaken but it won't hurt to give them another mixing." He handed Peg's box to Frawley. "Shake yourself a good piece of land, Mr. Trustee, and hand the box on to Mr. Dalton."

"Why now," Frawley said, "if I shake myself a good piece of land, Dalton there will shake it back down."

A man in the front row laughed, a tight, high laugh, almost a giggle, the kind of laugh that comes out of a man when his nerves have become so taut they must have release. It became a contagion, sweeping through the crowd like a spring wind. Men roared and slapped each other on the back and wiped the tears out of their eyes.

"It wasn't funny," Purdy mused. "It's just men getting their feet on the ground after being up in the air. A good study in crowd psychology, Murdo."

Gardner took Peg's box and handed Jewell's to Frawley. Peg said something, and for the first time Frawley seemed aware of her. He shook the box and passed it to Dalton, his eyes on Peg, frankly admiring her.

Dalton and then Jale Miller shook the box and Gardner placed it in front of Jewell. "All right, Miss Clancy." Gardner paused dramatically. "Make the first draw."

Jewell's hand slid through a small opening in the side of the box. She drew out a slip and read, "Hans Schottle."

"Hans Schottle," Gardner called, motioning for a secretary behind him to write the name on the long sheet of paper before him. "Now the tract, Miss Royce."

Peg drew a slip and read, "Tract Number 3,956, 20 acres."

"Tract Number 3,956, 20 acres," Gardner called. "Make your bid, Mr. Schottle."

A paunchy man near the middle aisle rose and called, "Two hundred dollars."

"I am bid $200," Gardner intoned. "Two hundred dollars. Two hundred dollars. Two hundred dollars for twenty good acres. Are you all done?"

"No." It was Short John Clancy standing on the left side of the tent, his buckaroos forming a tight knot behind him. "I bid $1,000."

Murdo Morgan stepped away from the platform, confidence draining out of him. This was Broad Clancy's trick, and Cole and his bunch were here to see that it worked.

# Chapter 22: Stampede

SILENCE GRIPPED THE CROWD. ONE THOUsand dollars! Broad Clancy had that kind of money. None of the settlers did. Fear was in them, then bitterness. The things that Royce and Blazer had said were right. Clancy would use his money to secure title to the land he had used for years.

For that one short moment Morgan didn't know what to expect and he didn't know what to do. He took an uncertain step along the platform, hand on gun butt, heard Gardner say, "Mr. Clancy, isn't that bid out of line with the value of the tract?"

"Hell, no," Short John bawled. "It's got our house on it. I ain't sitting here and letting some clodbuster named Hans Schottle have it."

"You're mistaken, Mr. Clancy," Gardner said. "Tract Number 3,956—"

Blazer was on his feet, bull voice roaring down Gardner's. "We told you boys what the company was, a damned thieving bunch of coyotes."

Royce jumped onto a bench and was shaking a fist at Gardner. "Look at him. Filling his pockets with honest men's money like he always has. Fixed it with the Clancys so you boys won't get the good spots the cattlemen want. You're just farmers. The company and the Clancys are in together."

"What about it, Schottle?" Blazer bawled. "You gonna stand for it?"

Morgan had started through the crowd toward Cole and his men, shoulder smashing a path, gun gripped in his right hand. He couldn't shoot in this packed mass, but if he could get to the men who were making the trouble, he'd silence them.

"Sure we're in cahoots with the company," Short John was yelling. "A purty penny it cost us, too. You saw it was my sister who pulled Schottle's name out."

There wasn't any sense in what Short John was saying, but it wouldn't take sense to turn these men into a pack of howling wolves. Blazer was yelling: "I'll get a rope. Swing 'em and let 'em dance."

Gardner was trying to talk from the platform, but his voice was lost in the rumble that rose from a thousand throats. Morgan got through the first two rows of men and no farther. The settlers closed up into a solid wall and began pushing toward the platform.

Blazer and the Sneeds with Cole and Royce behind them were jamming their way to the end of the benches toward the canvas, Blazer bellowing, "Wait'll I get a rope." Morgan couldn't reach them. He was being shoved toward the platform, the distance between him and Cole steadily widening.

Through a sudden lull in the roar of the crowd, Morgan heard Jewell's voice: "You were lying, John. Tell them you were lying." Morgan looked back at the platform. Jewell was on the ground trying to reach Short John. Now, as Morgan looked, she went down.

In that moment Murdo Morgan became a madman. He wheeled toward the platform, his gun barrel a terrible slashing club. Men spilled out of his way, cursing and crying out in agony. He was in the clear then. Dalton had seen Jewell and was bellowing, "Look out, you fools. You'll tromp the girl to death."

Morgan jumped to the platform and raced along it. Gardner and his office crew had picked up chairs and lined the edge of the platform to hold the settlers back, a thin line that would have broken under the mob's weight the minute it surged across the platform. Dalton and Frawley were fighting their way toward Jewell when Morgan took a long flying leap into the crowd, the swinging gun barrel opening a path for him. Dalton kept crying, "Look out for the girl."

Something stopped the forward push of the crowd. Morgan never knew what it was, Dalton's voice or his own gun barrel or the fact that Blazer was not there to urge them on. The settlers stood motionless, bewildered, those in front of Jewell breaking away from her. Then Morgan saw that Purdy was already there, Jewell on the ground below him. His face was battered, his nose was bleeding, his glasses torn from his eyes, but his gun barrel had been as formidable a weapon in his hands as Morgan's had been. Somehow he had kept them away from Jewell.

"All right, all right," Dalton and Frawley were shouting. "Sit down. We'll see if anything's wrong."

Slowly the crowd fell back. Men looked at each other, not sure why they had done what they had. Morgan lifted Jewell's still form in his arms, his high-boned face contracted by the passionate fury that was in him. He called: "I'm taking her to the doc. If she ain't all right, I'm coming back. You and all the land in hell ain't worth her little finger."

That finished it: Jewell's head resting against Morgan's chest, her face white, her wheat-gold hair cascading around her face. Shame was in them then. They sat down, the only sound in the big tent the shuffling of feet and squirming of bodies as they found their benches. Purdy said evenly, "Clancy, you're under arrest for inciting a riot."

Morgan was striding down the middle aisle carrying Jewell when he heard Gardner call, "Clancy, tell these men you were lying when you said you were in cahoots with the company."

"All right, I lied." Short John's voice was high-pitched and laden with fear. "We fixed it with Ed Cole. . . ."

That was all Morgan heard. He was out of the tent, running around the back of the store and across the street and along the front of the Silver Spur to Doc Velie's office. He kicked the door open, and Velie, rushing out of the back, bawled, "What the hell's going on—" Then he saw Jewell and said: "Here, Morgan. On this cot. What happened?"

Morgan told him while he made his examination. Velie said then: "No bones broken and I don't think she's hurt. I'd say she got cracked by somebody's fist and was knocked cold. You never know what happens in a mess like that."

"Do something," Morgan cried. "Don't stand there like a damned fool."

"All right," Velie said crustily. "I'll do something if you don't shut up. I'll hit you over the head and let you see how you come out of it."

Morgan subsided. He looked at Jewell's white face, a great emptiness opening inside him. She was breathing softly and evenly. Then she stirred and her eyes came open.

"You're all right?" Morgan bent over her, hand touching her face. "You're all right?"

"I'm all right," she breathed. "Is it . . ."

"Everything's fine." Morgan choked and turned

away. "Keep her there, Doc. She's not doing any more drawing."

The drum of running horses came to Morgan when he reached the street. He raced along the boardwalk to the Silver Spur. He saw them on the road to the north rim, five riders, dust rolling behind them. It was Ed Cole and his bunch, their horses on a dead run. He started toward the stable for his black and knew it would take too long. There were horses racked along the street. He wheeled toward a buckskin when Purdy came around the store, Short John Clancy in front of him, gun prodding his back.

Morgan's place was in town. This was what it would take to set old Broad off. "You're raising hell," Morgan said, swinging in beside Purdy.

Purdy peered at him, pale eyes blinking. "I aim to," he said. "You know how close that was?"

"I know how close it was for Jewell," Morgan said bitterly. "You saved her life, Abel."

Purdy didn't say anything until the cell door locked behind Short John. He fumbled in his desk until he found another pair of glasses and put them on. He sat down as if suddenly and terribly tired. "Nobody needs to thank me for what I've done, but I've been wanting to thank you. Broad Clancy didn't build his walls high enough. Time caught up with him. Nothing can stop the land sale now. Cole's bunch came back with ropes, but they were mighty surprised when they looked into the tent. They turned around and vamoosed without a word."

Purdy wiped blood from his face and wadded up his handkerchief. "I was in hell when you came, Murdo. Lost my guts. Sold out to Clancy like the rest of them, but the difference with me was that I knew better. Jewell and I used to talk about things before you came."

Turning in his swivel chair, Purdy reached for his pipe. "I'll never be the same again. Neither will the valley. I wasn't proud of myself six months ago. I am now. I've quit telling myself I'm doing the only thing I could. Security!" He laughed shortly as he dribbled tobacco into his pipe. "It's a bad bargain when anybody sells out for an intangible thing called security. Now you get over to the tent and stay in town. This isn't finished."

"What about the Turkey Track hands who were with Short John?"

"Rode out. Went to tell Broad about it, I guess."

Morgan returned to the tent, not fully understanding what had gone on inside Purdy but feeling a little of the new pride that was in the man. Gardner was on the platform, talking in a low tense voice, but it was so quiet that his words came clearly to Morgan in the back.

"That's the story of Josh Morgan and his boys who are buried at Jim Carrick's place. It's the story of what Murdo Morgan has tried to do for you, but that part of the story won't be finished until your hands are on the plow handles and you've turned the soil of this valley. You've repaid Morgan by suspicions and . . . well, I don't need to tell you what you've done. If you'd boiled over this platform a while ago the way you intended and messed up our records and maybe hanged Morgan and me, you'd have finished the land sale. That was what Ed Cole and Broad Clancy have been working for. They played it smart and took you for suckers. Now let's get one thing straight. What's it going to be from here on in?"

Frawley faced Gardner. He said without hesitation: "There will be no more trouble of our making, Mr. Gardner. Let's go on with the drawing."

"That's what I want to hear." Seeing Morgan in the back, Gardner called, "How's Miss Clancy?"

"Doc said she was knocked out. She'll be all right."

"Then we have something to be thankful for. Frawley, one of you trustees will have to draw in place of Miss Clancy."

"I will," Frawley said, and took the chair beside Peg.

"Clancy withdrew his bid on Tract Number 3,956," Gardner said. "Are you all done? Sold to Hans Schottle for the contract price of $200. Schottle, come to the rear of the platform, pay

280

the balance, and receive your papers. All right, Frawley."

Frawley lifted a piece of paper and read, "Joseph Ramsay."

Peg drew and called, "Tract Number 899, 40 acres."

A man in the back shouted, "Two hundred dollars."

"I am bid $200 for Tract Number 899," Gardner intoned. "Two hundred dollars. Two hundred dollars. Two hundred dollars for forty good acres. Are you all done? Sold for the contract price of $200. Who is the buyer?"

"Joseph Ramsay."

"Come to the back of the platform and pay your balance and receive your papers. Next, Mr. Frawley."

Morgan turned away. From now on it would go like clockwork. He walked back to Velie's office.

"She's all right," the medico said. "She went over to the hotel."

Morgan drifted aimlessly along the street, watching the clouds rush in from the southwest, smelling the pungent sage scent that was swept in by the damp breeze. It was raining now in the Sunsets and probably on west to the Cascades.

At noon Morgan met Peg and took her to dinner in the tent restaurant.

"Dalton's got my place while I'm eating," she said.

"You don't need to go back. After what happened . . ."

"I told you the platform was a good place to watch from." She spooned sugar into her coffee, eyes not meeting Morgan's. "I'm glad it happened. I've got some things straight now. You see, I never liked Jewell. She had the things I didn't, and they were the things I thought I wanted."

She raised her gaze to Morgan's face. "Maybe I had more fun than Jewell did, but fun isn't so important. I could have gone to San Francisco with Cole, but I didn't. I loved you. It's all right, Murdo. I didn't get the winning hand, but I got a good one. I'll marry Buck. I'll make him happy and I'll make Jim like me."

Purdy had said, "Time is a great sea washing in around us." He might have added that it changed people as it washed in. These months since Morgan had returned to the valley had been violent ones, twisting and shaping and melting human souls in life's hot crucible, but no one had changed more than Peg Royce. Looking at her now, Morgan felt an admiration for her he had never felt before. She was smiling, as if pleased with herself and her life. She had no regrets.

"What happened to you?" Morgan asked.

"Two things," Peg answered. "I know Jewell now and I like her. I like courage in anybody, and she had all the courage in the world when she headed into that crowd."

"The other thing?"

"I saw your face when you crossed the platform to her. She's your final woman, Murdo. Don't let her go."

"Her father happens to be Broad Clancy," he said bitterly.

"You crazy fool! It doesn't make any difference who her father is if you love her."

Maybe he was a crazy fool, but it did make a difference. That was the way life had dealt the cards, and it was beyond his power to change the deal.

Morgan went back to the tent with Peg, watched the drawing, and drifted away. Finding Ed Cole was his job, and he didn't know where to look. The man wasn't finished; he wouldn't be finished until he was dead. Cole would find Clancy, and the Turkey Track man would throw his crew in with Cole's.

Putting himself in their position, it seemed to Morgan that their natural move was to break Short John out of jail. The next would probably be an attack on the settlers' camp. The situation had become critical for Clancy and Cole, and they were the kind of men who would make a desperate move, now that failure had blocked their progress.

The drawing was closed at nine o'clock, the money locked in the safe of the Stockmen's Bank. Gardner said: "They'll try the bank,

Morgan. If they can get your money, you can't pay the Citizens' Bank and it will get the grant."

"By that time the land will be sold," Morgan said. "If that was Cole's idea, he'd wait till the finish, but we'll put the Carricks in the bank just to be sure."

Morgan cruised the street, tense, ears keening the night breeze for any sound that was wrong. He wanted to see Jewell, but he had kept away from her after she had gone to the hotel. If he saw her, he would tell her he loved her, and he shouldn't. Not yet. Not until it was finished. Perhaps he never could. Not if Broad Clancy died before his gun.

It was black dark now except for the transient veins of lightning that lashed the sky. Clouds had wrapped a thin moon and the stars in a thick covering. Thunder was an irregular rumble, growing louder with the passage of time. By midnight the settlers were asleep, their fires, dying red eyes in the night.

Jim and Buck Carrick were guarding the bank; Purdy was awake in his office, an array of rifles and hand guns on his desk. The waiting pressed Morgan, tightened his already taut nerves until every sound in the darkness made him jump and sent his hand dropping to gun butt.

It was nearly dawn when Morgan stepped into Purdy's office. "I'll be singing to myself if this doesn't crack," he growled, "and I don't sing worth a damn."

Purdy leaned back in his chair, forehead worry-lined. "Why are you so sure they'll move in tonight?"

"I know Broad. Cole is the kind who might quit, but not Broad. It's like Jewell says. It's all or nothing with him."

"But why tonight?"

Morgan jerked a thumb at the cell door. "There's your answer. Broad's got patience. He's let it play along, gambling that the ruckus at the drawing would do the job, but it didn't work. Now Short John's in the jug. That's too much for a Clancy."

Purdy nodded. "I told you this morning it was an interesting study in mob psychology. Do you know why that bunch didn't rush in like Cole and Clancy expected?"

"No. I've wondered about it all day. They acted like they was only half convinced."

"That's it. You swung them your way when you made your talk. They couldn't swing back fast enough. If Clancy and Cole could have pulled that off sooner, it would have been a different story."

"It was time we had luck." Morgan turned to the door. "I'm going to ride out to the camp. I should have told Dalton to put out a guard."

Morgan got his black from the stable and rode

around the Silver Spur and past the haystacks to Dalton's wagon. The three trustees were crouched around the fire, and when Morgan rode up, they rose. Frawley said, "Get down, Morgan. I couldn't sleep, thinking about what happened when you started the drawing, so I got Jale and Clay out of bed. We'd like to make it up—"

A gun cracked to the south. Then another. Men yelled and thunder rolled into the man-made racket. Morgan's head lifted. A new noise washed in on the night wind, a noise he had not heard for years. The rumble of many hoofs beating into the dirt.

"Stampede," Morgan cried. "Get everybody out of bed."

He swung his black around the wagon and cracked the steel to him, fear for the settlers' safety freezing his insides. This was Broad Clancy's ace in the hole.

# Chapter 23: Final Woman

A SLIVER OF PALE SKY SHOWED WHERE THE clouds broke away from the moon. Then it closed and it was completely dark again and thunder came with gun-sharp nearness. It began to rain, great slapping threads that plopped into the earth. Lightning scorched the sky as Morgan swung his black toward the leaders.

Morgan could not think nor plan. He could only pray that he would be able to turn the herd. At such a time man is a puny thing, dependent for life on the God above and the horse between his legs, but he gave no thought to his own danger. The safety of hundreds of settlers rode with him this night, settlers who had cursed and reviled him and hated him, settlers who had believed Royce's and Blazer's lies and accused him of treachery.

Four thousand hoofs! A million pounds of bone and muscle and horns! An avalanche of destruction, sweeping toward the camp. Ahead were women and children, innocent bystanders who would be crushed to death because of the inhumanity of a few greedy men. Women and children who had been brought here by their husbands and fathers, men who had followed a dream half the width of a continent, men who had committed no greater crime than to challenge Broad Clancy for the land he had used, land he did not own, land for which he had not even paid a paltry rent.

The last bit of restraint went out of Murdo Morgan. He had had opportunities to kill Broad Clancy. Now he regretted those chances which had been lost, but he could not honestly blame himself. Clancy was a proud and greedy man, selfish and arrogant, a man who long ago had driven Josh Morgan from the valley and brought death to his older son. Still, there had been some hint of restraint in him.

Morgan had not blamed Clancy for any part in the trap Cole had laid for him in the tules of Paradise Lake. He had never considered Clancy as a wholesale killer who would murder hundreds of innocent people to secure his own ends. Now, Morgan thought, he had been giving Clancy credit he had not deserved. The man must have planned this from the first as his final brutal stroke that could not fail, or he would not have brought a herd of this size to the valley from the summer range.

Morgan was in close now, the black's speed matching the speed of the lead animals. Morgan fired and a steer went down. Powder flame streaked into the night, the noise of the explosion lost in the thunder above and the thunder of hoofs beside him. The blazing ribbon that lashed from gun muzzle was no more than a match spark in a world lighted by cracking flashes.

Pull trigger. Throw bullets into the lead steers. Load and shoot again until the gun is empty. Press and push and hope that the raging line of beef can be turned away from the camp ahead. Hope that the black would not find a hole and fall, for only death awaited a rider who went down beneath those driving hoofs.

It was wild and primitive, a world without order. Chaos had broken loose. It was murder rolling across an earth that trembled under those hoofs, with only one man holding a small chance to avert tragedy, a slender reed in this gusty gale sweeping out of the gates of hell.

Morgan rode low in the saddle, his black straining under him, conscious only of the camp ahead, the diminishing distance between it and the herd, of time that was spinning out into eternity, of this balance between life and death. He could not let himself think of what would happen if he failed, of bloody bodies beaten into the mud, bodies that would not be recognized by those who loved them.

Seconds became minutes and minutes ran on into other minutes, and Morgan could not tell if he was succeeding or not. He knew that time was running out, that the campfires were closer, but those thoughts were loosely held in the fringe of his mind. There were just two things clutched in his frenzied consciousness: this roaring wave of destruction beside him, the swaying backs, the lumbering bodies, the rising and falling hoofs, all melting together into a single maelstrom of horror; the other, the result of failure that would sour his soul the rest of his life.

It was a black world that shook under him, lighted by flashing streaks above, pierced by ribbons of gunfire as he made his puny effort to shape destiny, a black and terrible world that permitted men like Broad Clancy and Ed Cole to bring this terror upon it.

Then the miracle! Other men riding out of the night. More guns to flash, more dead steers to fall along the danger edge so that this black, heaving horde would be turned, more men to yell and strike with coiled ropes and press the guiding end of the line, more men to help turn the steers into the empty land where they could run until they could run no more. Then there would be safety when breath was gone and hearts could no longer pound movement into those lumbering bodies.

The pressure was enough. The line turned, the direction changed. Not much, but enough. Away from canvas-topped wagons, away from camp-fires that had been replenished with dry wood and raced upward into the rain with sizzling banners of flame, away from the agonized cries of mortal terror as women and children tumbled over each other and fell and got up to run again toward safety.

Wagons flashed by. The town was behind. Somewhere out there in the vast and empty land the steers would stop when they could run no more.

Morgan reined away and let them thunder past. He pulled up and stepped down, a sudden weakness in him. Only now could he breathe, could he let his mind turn to what might have happened.

He wiped sweat from his face and gave thought to what had to be done. He loaded his gun, punching the shells into place with slow deliberate motions. There could be no turning back, no hesitation, no thinking of his personal feelings about Jewell. Broad Clancy had to die. He could understand what Cole had done to remove him, but he could not understand, now with the stampede roaring on to a harmless disintegration, what kind of satanic promptings had caused Clancy to start it. He did not try. His mind came to a wall of decision and stopped. This would not happen again with Clancy dead.

Daylight was washing out across the valley now. It had been no great space of time since the stampede had started, as time was measured by a clock, but in Murdo Morgan's life each minute had been an eternity.

Most of the riders who had helped turn the herd were staying with it, but they had pulled away and had slowed their mounts. Then Morgan saw two men wheel their horses and ride directly toward him.

For a time Morgan thought the riders were Broad Clancy and Short John, but the light was thin in the misty air, and when they were closer he saw that they were not Clancys. They reined up, one saying: "You'll have no trouble with us, Morgan. Put away your gun."

"Where's Clancy?" Morgan demanded.

"Short John's dead," the rider said tonelessly. "Broad may be by this time."

Morgan asked, "What happened?" his mind gripping this news and failing to understand it.

"We broke Short John out of jail," the buckaroo said. "Purdy got tagged, but he ain't hurt bad. We heard the stampede soon as we pulled out of town. We ran into Cole's bunch at the edge of camp and Broad cussed Cole for starting it. Cole said they aimed to bust up the settlers' camp. Broad called it murder and pulled. Royce got him. We drilled the Sneeds after one of 'em plugged Short John. Cole sloped out with Royce and Blazer. Broad told us to turn the stampede away from camp."

Morgan stared at the men, rain lashing his face. Slowly his gun slid back into leather. He had been entirely wrong about Broad Clancy. He did not doubt the truth of the story. This was not a time when a man could lie.

"We'll slope along," the rider said. "Broad wanted us to tell you. He's in town now, but he'll cash in before the day's over. A couple of the boys took him to the hotel."

"Thanks," Morgan said, and mounting, let the black take his own pace to town.

It was full daylight when Morgan reached Irish Bend. The storm was over. He rode slowly along the street, saw Broad Clancy's chestnut racked in front of the hotel and dismounting, tied beside him.

There was a strange stillness upon the town. Morgan remembered the hot spring day when he had first returned to the valley, a day that now seemed years ago. There had been silence then, the hostile silence with which Broad Clancy's Irish Bend welcomed strangers. This was different, a brooding silence filled with human fears.

Morgan sloshed through the mud to the wet walk and stood there a moment. The sun broke through the shifting clouds and gave a hard brightness to the street. Steam curled up from the soaked earth and roofs and boardwalks, and strong and pungent desert smells flowed around Morgan.

No one else was on the street. No horses were racked along it but the two in front of the hotel. A rooster crowed from somewhere back of Doc

Velie's office, the shrill sound beating into the silence. Then the stillness was upon the town again. It was as if nature, outraged for so long by the plots and counterplots of scheming selfish men, had decreed this day would see the end.

Morgan paced toward the bank. Peg Royce, stepping out of the hotel, called, "Murdo. Come inside."

He stopped, asking, "Where's Cole?"

"In the Elite. Blazer's with him. Jim Carrick shot Royce. Jim's hit, but he'll be all right."

The Elite was straight ahead, past the bank and across the side street. The instant Morgan rounded the bank and came into view, Blazer and Cole would cut him down. He stood motionless, considering this. He asked, "Where's Buck?"

"In the bank."

It would have been like Jim Carrick to stay where he had been stationed until the danger was over, but it wasn't Buck's way, and Morgan disliked the idea of young Carrick being behind him. He went on, seeing no way he could change it. Peg ran after him and caught his arm.

"They'll kill you, Murdo," the girl pleaded.

He shook her off and kept on until he reached the corner. There he pressed against the bank wall and shouted: "Ed! Come out or I'm coming after you."

"Wait, Murdo." Peg stepped into the bank. "Buck, Morgan needs help."

Cole did not answer Morgan's call. Morgan drew his gun and sent a shot through the side of the saloon. "Come out, Ed. You, too, Blazer."

Buck Carrick, inside the bank, laughed. "Why should I help Morgan, Peg?"

"I won't marry you unless you help him."

Morgan heard young Carrick's long breath. "You'll marry me if I help Morgan?"

"I promise."

"Don't, Peg," Morgan said without turning. "I'll wait 'em out."

"Shut up, Morgan," Buck said hotly. "I'll make my own bargain. Peg, I thought you loved Morgan."

"Not any more, Buck. You'll never regret it. I promise. Jim won't, either."

"Don't Peg," Morgan said again. "Don't throw yourself away on a man you don't love."

Morgan lunged into the street, gun in his hand. He was in the open, mud sucking at his boots. He was across to the other walk, then. He had floundered and splashed, expecting to hear shots, to feel the slamming impact of lead, but there was only silence.

From the alley back of the Elite, Morgan heard the crash of something heavy, perhaps a log, against the back door of the saloon. He took another step and slipped on the wet boards. He regained his balance, and that was when Blazer and Cole came charging through the batwings.

295

Morgan did not understand it. There was no time to consider it. Blazer's gun was in his hand. He fired, wildly, and began to run toward Morgan as if he had to end it now. This was the end, and Blazer recognized it. All the defeats he had suffered must have goaded him with their memory into this senseless lurching run.

Blazer slipped on the steaming boards as Morgan had a moment before. He fell, firing a second time as he went down, the slug slapping into the bank building across the side street. Morgan shot as the big man fell, and missed. Blazer lifted himself to his knees and leveled his gun, an animal-like wildness mirrored in his face. Morgan fired a second time, the bullet knocking Blazer off his knees.

Morgan held his position, hammer back, while Blazer battled death. He laid in a half-curl on his side, blood a spreading stain on his shirt. He tried to lift his gun; his breath was a liquid gurgle, and scarlet froth was on his lips. Then strength was gone from him and he rolled over on his stomach and laid full out, his hat falling from his head to lie, crown down, in a puddle of blood.

Now Ed Cole, still back in front of the bat-wings, was jerking frantically at his gun. It came out from under his coat, pathetically slow, for this was not his game. He was scared. It was there in the ghastly pallor of his face, in the twitch of his lips. He had depended on Arch Blazer, and the big man had failed him.

There was no guile now in Cole's blue eyes nor on his handsome face. Morgan read frustration in him, and a great great rage, and the fear of a timid wolf that was brave as long as he was with his pack, and now, separated, knows that his running days are over.

Morgan's gun was lined on Cole, finger slack against the trigger. Thoughts raced through his mind, thoughts of this man he had called friend, memories of the past when they had fought side by side, of his visit in Cole's San Francisco office, and the loan Cole had obtained for him.

"Shoot him," Peg screamed. "There's nothing in him worth saving."

Cole's gun was shaking while he raised it. Other memories flooded Morgan's mind; of the stampede, of the women and children in the settlers' camp, of his decision to kill Broad Clancy when he had thought Clancy had been responsible for it. He had seen stampedes, the bloody shapeless things that had been men before they had gone down under the hammering hoofs.

Cole fired. Morgan felt the breath of the bullet on his cheek. Then he squeezed trigger, and the sound of it was the slamming down of an iron curtain at the end of the final act. Cole dropped his gun, hands gripping his shirt front. His lips framed a word, but the sound that came from his throat was not a word.

The agony of death was in Ed Cole's face. Shock was there and disbelief, as if he had been sure through all of it that he would never be brought to this place. He fell across the walk, his blood a widening pool on the wet boards.

Then Dalton and Frawley and Gardner and a dozen other settlers boiled through the batwings to form a circle around the bodies, and Morgan understood.

"We were forted up behind the saloon," Dalton said, "waiting for some more of the boys, but when we saw you cross the street, we knew we had to do something, so we slammed the back door in." He scratched his chin, staring down at Cole. "Damned queer. Him and Clancy both had more'n they needed, but it wasn't enough. Now they ain't got nothing but a hot spot in hell."

Morgan asked, "Why did Cole stop to fight?"

"He couldn't get away," Frawley answered. "Royce got hit when they tangled with Clancy's bunch and they brought him to the doc. Jim Carrick blowed Royce's brains out and we threw a circle around the town. Cole and Blazer holed up in here."

Perhaps it was that way, but Morgan knew how it was with a man after he'd schemed and failed and run. Any man can run so long. Then he can't run. It had to be ended, one way or the other, and Ed Cole had died like a man.

"Thanks," Morgan said.

He put his gun back in his holster, suddenly tired and a little bitter. These men didn't understand. They never would. They had not tried to fight until this morning, but fighting was what he was made for. There would always be the little men who needed their fighting done for them. That was the way the world moved forward. Only now and then would he find a Jim Carrick or an Abel Purdy who had within his soul the courage to stand and fight.

"Why," Frawley said, pleased, "I guess you've got no reason to be thanking us. Not after what you've done."

"We'll get the drawing started, Morgan," Gardner said.

It didn't seem important to Morgan then. The important part had been done. He said, nodding at the bodies, "Take care of them," and turned away.

Buck Carrick was standing in front of the bank, his arm around Peg. When Morgan crossed the street to them, Buck tried desperately to hold his dignity: "Why'n hell didn't you wait, Morgan? I'd have given you a hand."

"I do my own snake stomping." Morgan stared at Jim Carrick's son who had hated him since that night at the Smith shack. "She's got no call to marry you, Buck, if she don't love you. She deserves something better."

"Now, hold on—" Buck began.

"I had some things wrong," Peg broke in. She stood tall and very straight, as cool and beautiful as carved ivory. "I lost my head about you, Murdo. Let's forget that. It was different this morning. I asked Buck to help you because I wanted him to own the land he lived on." She smiled and added: "The land I'm going to live on, Murdo. Broad died a little bit ago. Jewell will want to see you."

Morgan, looking closely at Peg, knew it was all right with her. Yesterday she had said she'd make Buck happy and she'd make Jim like her. She had meant it then and she meant what she said now. He went on, the desire to sleep a million years pressing him, but he couldn't sleep yet. Funny, the way it had gone. All the time he had been afraid he would have to kill Broad Clancy. Then Jewell would have been beyond his reach, for that was a thing even love could not have bridged. But Clancy had died before the guns of Ed Cole and his men.

He was in the hotel lobby then, and Jewell was behind the desk, as she had been that first day he had seen her. Stopping, he looked at her and thought of the things he had noticed then, of the eagerness in her blue eyes, her quick-smiling lips, her throaty laugh. But nobody had laughed much lately in Paradise Valley. The years ahead would be different. There was need for laughing, and there would be time for it.

"Dad's dead," she said. "Everything he had wanted was gone, but he said to tell you he hoped you didn't hate him. He brought that herd down to run through the big tent if everything else failed. He would have burned the town and your records and he aimed to kill you and Gardner, but he couldn't stand for Cole stampeding the cattle into the camp. He said he had never fought women and children. He was honest in what he believed. You believe that, don't you, Murdo? You can forgive him for what happened to your father and brothers, can't you?"

"Yes. I didn't come back to get square, Jewell."

She had not been crying, but now there were tears in her eyes. She rubbed them away and said a little angrily: "I know, Murdo. I'm not crying for him. I'm crying because of what he might have been and what he might have done. I think he saw it himself that last minute. He said he had lost Rip. He lost me. He made Short John come to the drawing to do what Rip would have done if he had been alive. Then he lost him. He didn't care if he lived or died. It was too late."

Morgan thought briefly of his own father who had dreamed his dreams to the last. He thought of Abel Purdy who had said that time was a great sea washing around them. Now everything was different. Looking at this girl who had missed so much of the goodness of life, he said, "It's not too late."

"What will you do now?" she asked.

"I kept back a piece of the butte land south of the valley. We could homestead the quarters between my land. Then we'd have patent to enough so we'd know we could hang on no matter what happens. Seems like this valley's got a big chunk of me. I'd like to stay here. Would you?"

"Yes, Murdo. That's what I'd like to do."

He came to her, and she moved away from the desk to meet him. He kissed her, and her lips were warm and rich. She had never given her love to anyone, but she gave it now, and Morgan, holding her in his arms, had a brief glimpse of the years ahead. They were inviting years, as winy and head-stirring as the cool thin air of the valley. She pulled her lips away and clung to him, her body hard against his; and in all the changes that the great sea washing in around them had brought, none were as fine as this.

Books are produced in the United States using U.S.-based materials

Books are printed using a revolutionary new process called THINKtech™ that lowers energy usage by 70% and increases overall quality

Books are durable and flexible because of Smyth-sewing

Paper is sourced using environmentally responsible foresting methods and the paper is acid-free

**Center Point Large Print**
600 Brooks Road / PO Box 1
Thorndike, ME 04986-0001 USA

(207) 568-3717

US & Canada:
1 800 929-9108
www.centerpointlargeprint.com